Praise for Else's writing:

"Else obviously has a vivid imagination and some of the story-telling passages are wonderful."
— Allen H. Peacock, Simon & Schuster

"his prose is evocative and he brings fresh sharp insight to family scenes"
— Deborah Futter, Bantam Doubleday Dell

" . . . some of your writing is beautiful. It is superb. You have tremendous talent."
— Sam Jordison, Galley Beggar Press*

"On Sunday February 23rd I suffered from insomnia and turned on the World Service in the middle of the night. I was absolutely captivated by what I heard. It was your short story 'Surviving on Mexican Shade'."
— John R Murray, John Murray Publishers

Else's fiction has been broadcast by the BBC World Service and included in a literary review published by the Sorbonne in Paris. His work *My Father's Lies,* which includes 'Surviving on Mexican Shade,' was shortlisted for the Shakespeare & Company Novella Prize.

* In December 2015 Galley Beggar Press will publish Else's story *First Kiss* as one of their monthly shorts, the story that inspired the First Kiss novels of which *Bathing with the Dead* is the first volume.

ELSE

Bathing with the Dead

Else

A Novel, that is, a work of fiction.

ISBN: 978-0-9965071-0-3

DEDICATION

Dedicated to my dear writer friends, Reine and Lidmila, who have read my work over the years and encouraged me to continue, to not give up, to tell my stories if only to them.

Look for Reine Melvin's wonderful book "Love and Water" coming out in 2016.

Look for Lidmila Sovakova's award-winning "The Drowning of a Goldfish" as well as her romantic Jazz Saga series, currently available.

BATHING WITH THE DEAD

A search for Love amidst lust, betrayal, enlightenment, embezzlement and murder in the oldest city in the world.

Volume One of the Else First Kiss series

Prologue

They would burn him, the two of them decided. For practice. Invite him to smoke from a spiked chillum pipe. Once the drug took hold they would wrap him in a death shroud, drench him with oil and pay to have the paralyzed still alive body cremated at Manikarnica Ghat. There, after three hours of hellacious burn, his anonymous ash would be spilled into the holy Ganges, removing all trace of the sacrificial act.

If this worked, if they were not found out, they would do the same with the one that mattered, with the American, the one whose disappearance could bring vast riches for them and a new temple for their patron God Ganesh, the elephant-headed Hindu God of wealth and fresh beginnings.

If only the other Gods were on their side as well. If only they could tell.

1 Randy And Fernanda

Randy loved Fernanda. He shifted in his seat as she dug her head deeper into the nook of his neck, her black hair streaming down his front. A chime sounded, the seatbelt light came on. Turbulence on their long flight to India. Who would have thought they would travel so far together? To such an exotic place, the oldest city in the world, Varanasi.

"You'll like it, you'll see," he told her. "Imagine a city on the banks of the Ganges, the holiest river in the world. People bathe in the Ganges, bathe their souls!"

He felt her grunt. Which made him smile. He loved even this, her stubbornness. Or were the calming capsules she'd taken earlier putting her to sleep? When he'd suggested she buy something for her fear of flying, he meant a strong sedative but she would have none of that. Only natural for her. She went to her herbalist, who suggested valerian root, two capsules before takeoff and then again every few hours. Yes probably the herb was drawing her down to sleep.

"I do appreciate you coming, Fernanda. I know you don't like to fly. And not being Hindu, the Ganges may be no more impressive to us than the Rio Grande with its wetbacks. But still." He forgot what point he was trying to make. "Anyway, it's a short project. My manager said the bank only wants someone to babysit the launch of their new system. A week, maybe two. What could go wrong?"

She grunted again.

He wrapped an arm around her. Pulled her closer. Her breathing slowed.

Randy first met Fernanda ten years before in a brothel club in Nuevo Laredo, Mexico. Her beauty and youthful energy captivated him as she played trumpet in the club band, in a balcony above the floorshow. Randy waved. She broke into a smile, pulled the horn from her lips, turned her face from him. He nudged his best friend Chance, tried to get his attention from the dancer on their table bouncing her naked breasts to the rhythm of the house band's song. "Chance, look!" he yelled in his ear. "Up there! The girl with the trumpet. I want to kiss that girl!" Which cracked Chance up. He hadn't driven 8 hours to Mexico to kiss some girl. That was no proper celebration of high school graduation. Chance had come to Mexico to drink, watch sex shows, and get laid!

Fernanda loved Randy. She tried to ignore the turbulence, tried to be still in her husband's arms. The pill helped. As for Varanasi, she'd never heard of the place until Randy asked her to accompany him there on this project. She had learned, in their first year of marriage, that even though Randy made his living as a traveling consultant for IBM, he hated travelling alone. Hated empty hotel rooms and pretending to befriend perfect strangers. The only thing that saved him, he told her, the only thing that made him a success in his ill-fitting profession, was that he put his heart into every project. He refused to fail. So, could she go with him this one time? Of course she could. Though she hated flying, she would accompany her dear Randy, save him as she had done that first night in front of the club in Boystown.

Dry lightning flashed in a distant thunderhead as seventeen year old Fernanda stepped, with her trumpet, from the sex club onto the dusty, neon-lit street of Nuevo Laredo's red light district. Closing time. Despite the dangers of such a place at such an hour, Father, as usual, would not walk her home. He was too busy pissing away his pay – on tequila, the drink, and Tequila, the one-eyed whore.

She noticed the American boy sitting on the curb across the street, the boy with the forlorn look. The boy who had waved at her earlier. In no hurry to cross alone the gloomy field that led home, she skipped over to him.

"Hola?" she said, tapping him on the shoulder with her trumpet.

He snapped up his head. "Oh. Hi."

"Why you still here?" she asked. "You need to go home. Party over."

His face looked like he would break into tears any minute - the drink and the long day's events apparently weighing on him. "I can't go home," he said. She liked his voice, liked his Texas drawl. "I'm broke and my friend Chance got arrested. He has the key." The American pointed to the lone car parked down the street.

She weighed the situation, feared what would happen to this American alone in Boystown all night. "Follow me," she told him. "My father's house is not far. You be my bodyguard tonight, yes? And sleep on patio."

The boy jumped up. "Are you sure your parents won't mind?"

"My father sleeps here in Boystown tonight. He is leader of the band." She steered Randy across a barren field, away from the ghastly red light, to a darkness pierced only by the sparkle of her eyes when she turned to him to speak. "My father," she told him, weaving before him in the dark, "my father is a viejo verde. A dirty old man."

The young American laughed. "I'm Randy," he told her. "A clean young man."

She laughed, turning her head to face him, flashing her cat eyes. "I'm Fernanda."

"Fernanda!" He touched her, felt her stir. "We've landed. We change planes here for Varanasi."

Randy noticed the other passengers staring when Fernanda stood in the aisle. He was proud to be accompanied by such a sensuous woman. The fact that she had abandoned him at the border after he smuggled her into the states when they were young, abandoned him to run off with his best friend Chance, well, that simply didn't matter anymore. Yes it had taken him almost ten years to win her back, still, that didn't matter either. All that mattered was that they were married, finally. Her love held his world together, now. Cemented their whole universe. Fernanda, the Mexican girl, adored her American boy and he loved her.

2 Bank Of The Dead

Fernanda cannot sleep. After the long flight and hectic ride from the airport, in a black taxi whose driver dodged cows, people, bikes and beautifully decorated trucks, by inches, after that trip of a dozen near misses and constant pumping of the brakes and honking of the horn, Fernanda's hands still tense from the anticipation of metal on metal or metal on bone, she tries to sleep but cannot.

She wonders how it is going with Randy, down to the bank to meet with the manager. She wonders how it is going with herself, feeling strangely adrift in the wake of Randy's doings, Randy's career. She fears a change is coming. She doesn't know why.

She studies the back of her hands, her nails, she needs to redo them. Needs to do so many things. Adrift, she feels adrift.

She climbs out of the creaking bed, takes up the guidebook and sits by the window. She tries to read but the words swirl around and make no sense. She sets down the book. Leans out the window of the hotel room overlooking the crowded steps that lead down to the Ganges. Wooden boats dot the wide holy river that flows as Himalaya snowmelt to the deltas of Bangladesh.

My love for you, Randy, is a river of snowmelt from the peaks of my loneliness. My love for you floods the earth, leaving me high and dry. For what is left of me if I give my all to you?

Why do such thoughts weigh on her, here, and now? Jetlag?

Yes, she is jetlagged, but in that peculiar way that tires you but will not let you sleep – and too the noise from below, the voices, the calls, in a language whose words she cannot understand but whose intent she cannot ignore – she must leave the room. Not for fresh air, no, there is none in Varanasi, only old air, older than life, full of dust and the smell of holy cow dung, fresh and dried. She leaves the room, walks the cramped hallway whose walls lean to the left, she leans too, and steps down with her feet in the grooved middle of the wooden steps, to the lobby where a girl is sweeping with a handful of straw the azure stone tiles. The door is open. Fernanda leaves the hotel, dodging a lingering cow whose deflated udder stretches to the ground. The cow's tail brushes Fernanda as she answers the call of the voices, of the crowd, of the humanity down on the stepped ghat where longhaired, bearded sadhu babas, holy grandfathers, in loose orange robes, sit longing for bliss, where children play and pilgrims buy cupped flower blossoms with candles to sail on the Ganges. Fernanda watches as a woman wrapped in a sari and a trailing silk shawl enters the water at the bottom of the steps. The woman's dark lined face becomes transformed, her lips part and her eyes widen. Just beyond the woman, male pilgrims stand in their underwear in the sluggish current, swirling their hands in front of them before dipping their heads. They have all come longing for a blessing, for Shiva's cure. Locals, along the shoreline, bathe and brush their teeth.

A burnt smell draws Fernanda's eyes downriver, past the skyline of old turrets, temples and hotels, where a black plume marks the site of the special ghat for the dead, a place with bodies smoldering on wooden pyres by the river bank, a staircase where ashes of the dead and unburned body parts are collected by Chandalas, by untouchables, and tossed into the river. From her guide book reading she imagines taboo-breaking sadhus seated alongside the burning dead, smearing their bodies with warm ash and toasting, from gnarly skulls, the grand illusion.

"*Dios Mio*, Randy. What have you got me into?"

3 Bank Of The Living

Randy chuckled as he approached The First Ganesh Bank of Varanasi, a veritable temple to money, dodging sidewalk marigold vendors and sleeping dogs. He could not help but be thrilled! Partly because his new wife, Fernanda, had agreed to accompany him on this trip, but more so because he loved the stimulation of exotic locales such as India. And this had to be the most unique venue he'd worked as an IBM consultant. Built in the bowels of an ancient temple, next door to an ashram for the dying and a bakery for the living, the place had a unique smell of incense, decay and fresh baked bread.

Yes, this short project at the temple bank in this, the oldest city in the world, along the banks of the holiest river, promised to be a most unique experience. Perhaps even more rewarding than the long project he worked a few years back, before he was married, at the Louvre museum in Paris, where he had digitized and data-stored the Mona Lisa and her companions. A professionally satisfying but personally unsettling period - he had tried and failed at love with a Parisian woman, a headstrong woman, a woman who still haunted his dreams. Julie...

Randy paused at the shrine to the brightly colored, flower-necklaced, elephant-headed God in a niche in the entrance to the bank. The hard stone-polished interior of the bank, the walls smooth and cool to the touch, contrasted with the beige rough sandstone exterior. This Hindu God, Ganesh, sitting before him, Randy had read up on him. Even bought a sandalwood-carved version at the airport in Delhi. The god of wealth and success. A natural fit he supposed for a bank, and a good idol to place on his mantel at home in Arkansas. Still it struck Randy strange, that a temple and a bank could be so combined. A crossing of some line – but maybe that was just his colonial mindset.

Randy noticed how the Hindus, upon entering, bowed low at the shrine, touching fingertips to the ground and then to their foreheads. He saw the obvious reverence they held for Ganesh. He wondered at the innocent fanciful nature of their faith, but then, the thought struck him, weren't all faiths basically the same. Flowers in the same bouquet? At the age of twelve his own Baptist faith was stolen from him by the emptiness he felt in doing religious acts by rote at church on Sunday.

"Why do we pray to God?" he dared ask his Baptist Sunday School teacher. "Why don't we just talk with him?"

"Praying is talking with him," replied his teacher, a middle-aged man with a mustache, dressed in his Sunday best.

The other boys in class looked at twelve year old Randy like he was an idiot.

"No," said Randy, scratching at the stiff collar of his own Sunday shirt. "Praying is talking *at* God. I want to talk *with* Him. Why can't we talk with God?"

"God answers, but not with words. He answers with feelings and deeds."

"Doesn't he speak English?" said Randy.

The other boys cracked up, making Randy feel the fool, but at the same time, deep inside, he sensed that he was on the right track and they were the lost ones.

The teacher shook his head, placed a hand on Randy's shoulder, telling him, "One day you will understand."

But Randy wasn't drinking that spoiled milk. Even at such an early age, he understood that he would never be satisfied worshipping God's footprints. He wanted to be in God's presence, talk with him, even. He did not know why he was different from others in this way. In a small part of his heart he wished that here, in India, God would find him.

Many of the Indians entering the bank had red dots smeared

on their foreheads, between their eyes, the old and the young; this made them look to Randy as if they'd been shot. And back from the dead. Or soon would be?

What a strange wonderful place to find himself. He went further into the chill ill-lit lobby of the First Ganesh Bank. He mingled with the crowd of customers. This bank-temple reminded Randy of the ancient objects in the Louvre, but it was living history, a living museum. He would help them as he could with his 21st century skills, his computer savvy and his adeptness at project management. But would he be up to the challenge of the project? He always had doubts going into a new project.

Dark men with slick black hair, in slacks and long-sleeve striped and checkered shirts, and women, both thin and full, dressed in saris, with long black hair and head scarves, formed lines before him. Deposits and withdrawals. Withdrawals and deposits. On the far wall Randy made out a brass sign with exotic flowing Hindi script and below, in English, the words "Bank Manager."

"Can I help you, sir?" asked a well-dressed short young woman, blocking his way to the door at the last moment, curiously cute despite her obvious underbite and heavily mascara-lined eyes.

"I'm here to see Mr Tishwali." Her eyes softened at the mention of the bank manager's name. "I'm Randy from IBM. Here to help with the new computer system." He showed her his IBM badge.

"We were not expecting you today, sir," she said. Her dark eyes batted.

"Yes, the flight was cheaper," he said. "I brought my wife with me." She didn't hear him, had already disappeared past the heavy wood door of the manager's office. She came back out momentarily and told him, "Please wait, Mr Tishwali is busy."

So Randy sat on a bench in the corner and remembered his last phone conversation with Mr Tishwali, bank co-owner and manager, the week before coming to India. In a booming voice the man had practically insisted that Randy bring his wife along for the trip.

"I want you to be happy while you are here in Varanasi working for me. How can a man be happy without his life companion?"

Randy agreed. But convincing his wife Fernanda had been another story.

Randy sat there with his hands in his lap, watching the bank customers and young tellers, busy doing their daily business. The business of their lives. He was an expert computer coder, Randy, but generally clueless when it came to business affairs.

Just then a bent, white-bearded man in dirty orange robes entered the bank. The man was a sadhu, one of the homeless holy men who live in cubby holes along the river. Randy watched as he practically rowed himself across the stone floor with a thick wooden staff. The people at the nearest teller window stepped back to allow the holy man in front.

The orange-robed man handed a paper to the teller, who appeared puzzled and called over a floor manager. The manager spoke reassuringly to the teller, and the next thing Randy knew, the teller was handing the crippled holy man a thick stack of bills which he placed in a fold in his robe. The holy man bowed to the teller and turned to leave.

Randy stood. For this transaction struck him as wrong. What's a homeless man doing withdrawing a small fortune from the bank? How could he even have an account here with more than a few rupees? Randy moved closer to take a good look at the man as he struggled toward the door. The peculiar cloudy eyes, the tanned creased face, his skull shaved except for a sprig of hair on top tied with a red ribbon. His eyes met Randy's for a moment, a certain pleading in them, almost as if he were asking Randy's permission to leave.

"Mr Randy?" the young woman's voice made Randy jump. "Mr Tishwali will see you now."

4 A Morning Walk Along The Ganges

Left or Right. Fernanda must decide, at the bottom of the steps from the hotel, her sandaled feet inches from the river's edge. The unsettling scent from the crematorium makes up her mind, she turns right, away from the burning dead. As she walks she notices how the character of the steps change, from thin to wide, from painted to plain concrete, from crowded to lonely. Obstacles abound, boatmen preparing to launch their craft, bed sheets from hotels spread on the steps to dry, pilgrims standing in bunched groups listening to their guide, a shirtless holy man seated in front of twenty others reciting prayers and eating a ritual breakfast.

"Caca, caca and more caca," Fernanda complains, dodging the piles of water buffalo and cow poop on the ghat she is currently strolling. Men strip to their underwear right before her, at the river's edge. They enter the river, swirl the green water then dunk themselves, once, twice, three times.

An orange-robed young man, with long hair and beard, wearing a beaded necklace, sits inside a portico eating with his bare hands a meagre meal of rice and vegetables. An older, similarly dressed man sits on the steps below him, contemplating the river, as the morning breeze plays with the folds in his robe.

Haven't they something more worthwhile to do than pray all day? wonders Fernanda. They wouldn't last a month in Mexico. She makes her way past the men, looking away from them, towards the river where a boy is learning to swim with the help of empty water jugs tied under his arms. She looks back at the two orange-robed fellows sitting cross-legged, idle hands in their laps, and shakes her head. Thank goodness Randy isn't a holy man.

She finds a piece of cardboard, and sits down on the steps. The Ganges, though wider, reminds her of the Rio Grande. Only the Rio Grande one swam not to cleanse the soul but to reach the land of plenty. Her own path to America had started with her determination as a teenager to finish her bilingual business studies, no matter the distractions like the boys who drove her to the river park where they kissed her and begged her to do dirty things. She missed not a single class her final year, even though she had to work late each night playing trumpet in her father's band. Her father drank like most Mexican men she knew, and had one lover after another, living only for the present – she lived then for the future, a future in a new land with a different kind of man than her father. A man who could be true to one woman.

5 Banking On The Past

In the Grand Palace, a 3 star hotel just up the street from the Asi Ghat and a few blocks down the street from the First Ganesh Bank of Varanasi, Julie, a young French businesswoman on apparent vacation, tried on her new Indian outfit. She loved the feel of the green silk, the way the embroidered, sequined pattern sparkled in the light. She spun in front of the mirror, as if she were a teenager, then caught herself in the glass with critical eyes. She had aged since she last saw him. Was that a wrinkle in the corner of each eye? Heartbreak does that.

Oh how memories of love gone wrong will drive you mad!

When Julie first met the American at Le Danton in the Latin Quarter in Paris, the American that later broke her heart, she was taken by, first and foremost, his smell. She had leaned close to hear him say something about a film, Cries and Whispers, and she noticed he smelled clean and fresh and something more, something she could not finger, though in her mind she got an image of baby's skin.

"Randy," she heard him say. He was named Randy.

She had trouble understanding, as they talked, concentrating as she was, the whole time, on where exactly the smell originated. Was it his hair, his breath, his neck, his chest, his crotch? She pretended to drop a coin, to see. But she could not pinpoint an exact source; his entire body simply smelled wonderful.

Having just recovered, at the time, from a nasty breakup with a lover, an affair that had nearly cost her marriage, she was certainly not looking for another adventure. But the Latin Quarter remained, since university at La Sorbonne, a favorite place for her to hang out. She loved the energy of the students and the tourists. Her soul fed off the spiritual weight of the buildings and cobbled walks hundreds, if not thousands, of years old. And yes she looked forward to chance meetings with interesting people. People like Randy.

Early on she explained to him, over wine, her theory about kissing.

"Kissing cements lovers," she told him. "Connects them in a way I can't explain."

"Yes, perhaps you are right, but . . ."

"So we can never kiss," she told him, placing her hands on his. "I already have a good French husband. You can only be my friend."

But the more time she spent with him, watching old films, walking streets haunted by artists and philosophers and lovers, living and dead, the more time she spent with him sitting in Le Danton discussing the possibilities of being in love without ever kissing, the more she found herself thinking of him. All the time. At work and at home. Even when she was with her husband.

And then of course, that incredible night when leaving a powerful film from a tiny theater near Git Le Coeur, he had cried like a child in her arms, in the middle of the street, and she let down her guard enough to go with him to a hotel there, and almost, almost they made love. She wished that they had made love. But she could not break her stupid rule of no kisses, and it appeared he could not perform without her kiss. A perfect deadlock. Which led to that fateful breakup at the flea market in the north of Paris. When she lost him, because she neglected to tell him that she was his after all. That he had won the right to her kiss.

How her heart had ached at the realization of his absence from her life, when he left Paris, when he left her to chase some old Mexican flame. How her heart ached still. All on a misunderstanding. He thought he could never win her when in fact she was his all along!

Months passed. She prayed each night that the crushing need she had for him would die. But it did not, only grew stronger; it seemed to multiply with every prayer she made. Until the need for him overwhelmed her. Suffocated her. She had to take action, to save herself. To save them!

She came up with an ambitious plan, using her years of project management experience. A plan to track him down, her American, to seduce him and win him back. To recreate the love they had had together in Paris. She spent every spare moment at the office, scouring the world for just the right project that her company could outsource to IBM. And finding that project at last, she insisted to her manager that she knew the perfect consultant for the job, one whose stellar work on the Louvre project spoke for itself.

That American fellow, that Randy they'd used on the Louvre project, he was the one they needed for the Indian banking project. She repeated the words until they became a kind of mantra in the office. He was the one they needed. The American.

For he was the one she needed, Randy and no other.

Now, here she was, in India, and here he was too. At least that is what the project manager had told her on the phone late last night. Randy was here and hers for at least 2 weeks! She observed the conflicted woman in the mirror, studied her looks and worried, worried that when he recognized her, when he first saw her on the street in India, that he would see through her plan immediately and laugh. The thought terrified her. "Mother Mary, don't let him laugh at me!" She opened the door to her room and stepped out into the warming morning of Varanasi in pursuit of the past.

6 Brahmin Brahma

The immobile Brahma bull, largely white with a black splotch across his back that spread over the high hump like a shadow rider, meditated in the middle of the street full of honking vehicles and pesky pedestrians. Despite the distractions and his own deep trance, he noticed the appearance before him of a French woman in festive Indian dress. For something about her shone.

"She is the one," announced a girl next to the bull, touching his shoulder. "You can see the love need in her, can't you? She is the sacrifice."

The bull, known in the neighborhood as Brahmin Brahma, was not surprised at the girl's sudden appearance, at her light touch on his thick skin, at her babbling about some sacrifice. No more than he would be at the bite of a mosquito, or the buzz of a fly. No doubt the girl with her sweet smile and burning hazel eyes was a temporal incarnation of Kali, Deva of seduction and castration. He wanted nothing to do with that mad Goddess. But despite this he opened his bulbous black eyes wider and took in the French woman's exquisite face, opened his deep black nostrils and sniffed her jasmine perfume as she crossed before him and the girl and continued up the street.

"You will help," the girl, Kali, said, reaching with her tiny hand, pressing a finger to his forehead, between his horns, marking him with a red dot of her own blood.

"You gods bore me," Brahmin Brahma said, speaking somehow through the magic of the red dot she'd placed over his soul. "I follow your rules of conduct, or whims should I call them, life after life. I observe the rituals and strive for holiness. Yet do I reach Nirvana? No, never. Time after time I die and reincarnate in another miserable body. Look at me this time! I am a stupid Brahma bull on the loose in Varanasi."

The girl shook her head in sympathy.

"True, Brahmin Brahma, you led a good past life," she said. "You were set for Nirvana, for the heaven you so deserved, but your son . . ."

"Oh so now it is our children's karma that denies us Nirvana?" he spoke out, surprised he would argue so with a Goddess.

"You were on your funeral pyre," the girl said walking around to his tail – he felt her with each swish. Tried to brush her away.

"Stay away from there," he warned her, ready to kick.

The flirtatious girl laughed and continued round his massive body. "All your son had to do to finish the funeral rites was to circle you three times with the eternal flame, then light your pyre." She started to circle him again. "Two times he made it around your corpse, but then he dipped the straw and the fire leaped at him. In panic he dropped the burning straw, dropped your chance at Nirvana, to save his own hand." She gestured as if she were pushing fire from her hand. She, the Goddess of black fire! "Your son failed you. If he had let his hand burn and completed three times round you with the eternal flame your cycle of rebirths would have ended. But two times," she showed him two with her little fingers, her fiery eyes burning into his, "Two only gets you the body of a bull."

"Humph," said Brahmin Brahma. He'd had enough of her lessons. He turned, engaged his hefty leg muscles.

"Wait," cried the girl. "I have a deal for you Brahmin Brahma. I will give you Nirvana at the end of this life. Guaranteed." She cupped her hands in offering. "I only ask you not to interfere, when the time comes."

"Humph," repeated the bull. He left the girl in the middle of the street, in the middle of honking cars, lumbering trucks and dodging motorbikes. He left hoping one of them would strike her down as he slow-walked to the river for a drink.

7 A Big Banana

Fernanda slips on a fresh cow patty and falls into a boat full of poor pilgrims, of bare feet and pooling water and a hundred dark eyes in weathered faces staring down at her. A woman with black teeth and a henna pattern veining her arms leans down, helps Fernanda to a spot on the splintered stern of the overcrowded vessel. Fernanda is entranced a moment by the pattern on her arms, by the gold chain running from her nose to her ear, and the red round dot on her forehead. Then she realizes the boat is moving. Fernanda stands, starts to get off, but the boat is too far from the concrete steps. She sits back down. She isn't about to jump into the filthy water of the Ganges - she can't swim. She decides to sit quietly and let fate take her where it will.

Water leaks into Fernanda's shoes. She smiles nervously at the woman with black teeth and tattoo and the nose chain and the dot between her eyes. The woman smiles back, puts her hands together in prayer fashion and bows slightly towards Fernanda.

Fernanda puts her hands together too and prays, prays that the boat won't sink; though after a while she relaxes and enjoys the sight of the crowded ancient ghats, now, from the relative sanitary safety of the vessel. Pressed all around by the warmth of the pilgrims.

She had not enjoyed walking the ghats, not at all! Walking in the midst of the hawkers, pilgrims and local men stripping to their underwear and less at the water's edge, the thin bearded unholy-looking men in orange robes staring into space, the teenage boys leering at her bottom, telling her they could get her anything she desired.

"I know," said one boy in a group of teens tailing her, "I know what you want. I bet you want a big banana!" He repeated this again and again, in an ugly accusing fashion. She tried to ignore him, outpace him, but he stayed after her until finally she turned on him, furious, shouting, "Yes I want a big banana! So why are you here? You with that string bean? Vayase al Diablo!" And just then she slipped on the cow shit which landed her in the lap of these pilgrims on a prehistoric boat.

Please let us reach Calcutta before we finish sinking, she prays, the water in the bottom of the boat now up to her ankles. Anywhere but back to Varanasi!

8 Lord Hanuman Watches From Above

"She is the one?" asked the all-devouring goat of Lord Hanuman, the monkey god, sitting atop the roofline of Varanasi, looking down on the tourist boat returning to the ghat from which it began the tour, the boat with Fernanda, Randy's strong-willed Mexican wife, whose unlined upturned face catches the morning sun and glows like a misplaced moon through the morning haze.

"I believe so," Lord Hanuman replied, thoughtful. "She is strong, beautiful, in love. But some would swear the other, the French woman. I cannot clearly see which of the two will be chosen. There could even be a tie."

"I don't like the sound of that," said the goat, crunching the paper body of a lost kite that had fallen on the rooftop. "No clear winner in this affair of the heart? No clear winner?"

"All love demands sacrifice. Of the highest order," reminded Lord Hanuman. "There will be a sacrifice. And this Mexican woman is worthy. At 17 she traded a kiss for a new life in America. Borders mean nothing to her."

A breeze kicked up, exciting a flock of swifts who swept out over the river and back to the upper corridors of the ghats, in and out of the courtyards and between the temple tops, swallowing mosquitos and gnats.

"And this young woman, this Fernanda, she spent years living with a boy named Chance, at a crystal mine near holy hot springs, absorbing all that psychic energy. She would make a wonderful sacrifice."

The devourer goat tried chewing the kite's cross of sticks, but spat it out.

"Well one of them, French or Mexican, will pay," said the goat. "The price of heart's desire is pain."

Lord Hanuman laughed. "The tide in such affairs can turn in a heartbeat." He reached over to his pet, brushed its bristly back hair along the knobbed spine with the rough black palm of his monkey hand. "We can only wait and watch."

"And if matters call for you to act?" the goat asked, "you who can lift a mountain with one hand, you who can swallow the sea?"

"For now let's watch and wait," Lord Hanuman repeated, curious to see how things would play out without his intervention.

9 The Illusion Of Money

Randy stood aside as the manager's door opened and 3 dark men in suits came out all smiles. He watched as they thread their way through the lobby crowd towards the exit, where they stopped and bowed to the God Ganesh.

"Come in! Come in!" A deep voice called from the office. Randy went inside, closing the door behind him.

Mr Tishwali, the bank manager of The First Ganesh Bank of Varanasi, a man as big as his responsibility, came round the desk to greet Randy. He was a large man, yes, with protruding eyes under bushy eyebrows. He had a thick nose and a mouth that trumpeted words rather than speak them. His long beard swayed like the trunk of Ganesh.

"Welcome, welcome, Mr Randy! Mr IBM!"

Impeccably dressed in a tailored, white linen suit, his manner indicated a careful man, a man who thought before he acted.

"Pleased to meet you, Mr Tishwali."

"You traveled far," said the bank manager. "Yet arrived a day early!"

Randy smiled. "Yes. Since I brought my wife, I caught the cheaper flight."

"Excellent! Of course I can't pay for her ticket. You did understand that? My mentioning your wife on the phone was only a suggestion. For your well-being. I can barely afford to pay your expenses, much less those of your wife!"

Randy forced himself to smile. He hadn't expected anyone to reimburse him for his wife's expenses, so Mr Tishwali's comments struck an off chord with him. Maybe all bank managers are like that? Penny-pinchers?

Mr Tishwali squeezed back behind the smallish desk, made smaller by Mr Tishwali's hulking figure.

In the wobbly chair in front of the desk, Randy took in the primitive diplomas and citations hanging on the walls, proclaiming Mr Tishwali's accomplishments. "Impressive," he said.

"They're fakes," confessed Mr Tishwali. "I printed them off myself. My new partners prefer to think that I know what I am doing. You saw their happy faces, yes? They are ready to invest in our expansion. 10 temple banks in the year to come. In five years we'll have a temple bank in every city. They are so pleased to see us upgrade our system to IBM. To know the deposits will be fully insured." He took a second to file away papers. "You see, I have to appear to know what I am doing." He rubbed his beard, a slight smile breaking through the hairs round his mouth. "Yet I don't, really. Know what I am doing. I make this life up as I go."

Randy sat numbed from the verbal barrage. "I see," he said finally, wanting to like this white-suited man but not really trusting him. "Is the new hardware and software installed?"

"Yes," said Mr Tishwali. "Your technicians have replaced our old IBM PCs with the new system. We've suffered without long enough." He turned his monitor towards Randy to show the new banking system login screen. "We've been awaiting the arrival of your excellency to begin using the new system." Mr Tishwali's watery eyes blinked.

"So what system are you running now, if the old one is gone?"

"Doing our business on paper ledgers this week. We'll reconcile the account entries when we start using the new system."

Randy thought he saw the wall move, realized it was a lizard, the same color as the wall, darting up to a crack where the wall met the ceiling.

"The world is full of strange stirrings and unexplained mysteries," said Mr Tishwali. "Take something as obvious as money.

I bet you think that paper money has value?"

"Yes, I suppose I do," said Randy, thinking, what a talkative, curious fellow.

"That's because you are not a banker," this elephant of a man proclaimed. "We bankers know better."

Randy could think of nothing to say to that; he felt himself slipping into the fog of jet lag.

"Don't think that when a person deposits money we keep it separate from everyone else's. We throw it in a pile. And mark a little credit in your bank account, a digital setting on a disk. That's all your money is, a cipher, an electronic scribble that could disappear like a tear in the rain. So what a blessing is the backup and auditing capabilities of this new system! As soon as we flip the switch we will be fully accredited. All our customer's deposits will be insured by the DICGCI."

"The what?" asked Randy, trying to shake his sudden malaise.

"The Deposit Insurance and Credit Guarantee Corporation of India. Like your American FDIC."

"Oh," said Randy. "And before you, they, were not covered?"

"Forget the past," he told Randy. "The future is everything! That's what I tell my partner. You won't like him. He is an Aghori sadhu. A kind of demon holy man. Converted when we were kids.

Remind me to tell you the story."

He leaned forward and waved a wide hand in front of Randy's half closed eyes. "Am I boring you?"

"Sorry," said Randy, stifling a yawn. "The long flight, you know." He stretched. "So when do you want the system to go live, Mr Tishwali?"

"Soon. It must be soon, Mr Randy!" He smiled largely, stood. "The clerks have already been trained by the dealer from Mumbai."

Randy nodded, standing himself. "Good."

"I do have a favor to ask?" said Mr Tishwali.

"Yes?"

"Besides watching over the system for the first week, I would also like you to teach my computer staff how to program. So they can make accounting reports and maybe one day even small changes. I can't afford to pay IBM for every little report change I need in the future."

"I hear you," said Randy. "Realize though there is only so much I can teach them in the time I will be here. I would recommend formal classwork for them after I leave."

They walked to the lobby and down a short corridor to a large room where cold, conditioned air blasted from a slot in the cinder block wall. A trunk-size computer with wires running to and from a patch panel sat in the middle of the room. At the control console huddled an Indian girl, the funny-looking one that Randy had met in the lobby. She rose as Mr Tishwali introduced them.

"Neelu, this is Mr Randy. He is going to teach you and Rakesh how to program our new system. Starting tomorrow."

Neelu was cute the way the runt in a Pekinese litter can be cute. She put her hands together and bowed slightly to Randy. He mimicked her motion.

As Randy followed Mr Tishwali up the corridor back to the lobby, he was startled to meet the eyes of someone in the crowd. Eyes so familiar, eyes that sparkled with recognition. But then the face disappeared in the crowd. Funny what can set off a memory, thought Randy. A certain smell, a lingering look from a stranger – suddenly you feel an ache, a forgotten longing. Suddenly your heart hurts and you can't put your finger on why.

Strange. Perhaps another symptom of jet lag? The six hour drive from Arkansas to Dallas, the interminably long flight from Dallas to Delhi, and then the long wait for the connection to Varanasi had exhausted him. Or maybe he was just hungry. He told himself he should break early for lunch. He liked basmati rice. Wondered if he could find a restaurant that made good basmati rice. And naan. He loved hot buttered naan.

10 Beauty Like A Flower Awaiting The Bee

"*Il est la!* He's here!" cried a joyous Julie as she twirled in her sparkling silk dress in the middle of the street in front of the bank. Her cry was lost to the honking and the hustle of midday Varanasi; only the street-side marigold and grape vendors watched her in wonder. She walked a block from the bank, super-excited. What should she do next? To meet in the bank would be too obvious. She waited instead in a shadow, next to a sleeping dog and an old woman who squatted looking out on another day with little hope of the new and remarkable.

Julie waited an hour, ignoring offers of oranges and green grapes from pushcart vendors. I am doing the right thing, she told herself. Good things in life don't just happen. You have to make them happen. Oh who am I kidding? This is all wrong. This plan of mine. I am an awful person. I won't do it. I'll leave now and never see him again. I'll let him live his life in peace. With that Mexican woman. She felt a pain in her heart at that thought. I should leave, she told herself, leave before it is too late, before I destroy us all.

Then she saw Randy come out from that temple bank, looking lost and lonely. She practically broke into a run straight towards him. Forced herself to slow down. Walk girl, walk. Good, he was heading her way. She walked slowly, hoping he'd look up and recognize her, but he didn't. He started to walk right past. She panicked, reached out and grabbed his shirt. *"C'est pas vrai! C'est toi? Randy is that really you?"*

Randy turned, puzzled, then recognition came. He remembered her, what she had meant to him, she could see it in his eyes. The love he'd once had for her.

"Julie? Julie? Oh my gosh Julie, what are you doing here? Are you on assignment too?"

"Vacation, Randy," replied Julie, her knees trembling. "I came for the festival of Holi. Last week. Such an incredible place, isn't it?"

Randy just kept shaking his head, obviously overcome by the reality of this impossible chance meeting.

"But what are you doing here Randy?" she asked. "Did you take part in the festival as well?"

"No. I didn't even know. I just arrived. I'm here for a project. At the temple bank there." He pointed. She looked at the bank for a second, then back into his eyes.

"What a small world, no?" she said. "And what a surprise! You here! Two years right? Such a miracle to meet like this!" For a moment she lost herself in his eyes, in a memory, a spring day, Paris. A sudden downpour, the two of them running into the Saint Severin cathedral, laughing like naughty children into the presence of God.

A cart full of toys wanted by them. A grunt from the vendor woke Julie from her reverie. They stepped out of the way.

"It's unbelieveable," said Randy, and Julie studied his expression, to make out what he meant.

"OK, I'll tell you the truth," she said, and for a moment she thought she was really going to do just that. "The truth is I work for the CIA and I've been trailing you for months now. You should see your dossier."

Randy laughed. "Am I so dangerous?"

"Only to those that fall for you," she said without thinking. An awkward silence passed. She knew she had to say just the right thing or she'd lose him forever. "Why don't we find a restaurant and catch up with each other's lives," she suggested. Her future happiness relied on his answer.

His smile reassured her. "I'd love to have lunch with you. Why don't you come back to my hotel – my wife Fernanda is waiting for me. We could all have lunch together."

The world, with all its saints and promise, came crashing

down around Julie. He'd brought his wife. Her legs threatened to fail her.

"Why did you do that? Why did you bring your wife?" Julie said, then caught herself. "I mean, this is not a place for everyone, so dirty, so poor."

"I hate traveling alone, so I talked her into it. But, you are crying," said Randy, reaching to her cheek and touching the tear's wet trail.

"It's just . . . I'm so happy to see you. Again. I thought I never would, after the way you left me, in Paris."

She wished she had never come up with the plan to reconquer Randy. She wished she could die.

"I had to leave you, to save myself," Randy told her, putting a hand on her shoulder. "Because I knew I could never have you." He took a step back from her, his eyes evoking memories that weighed on her as well.

"You don't understand. You DID have me! If you'd only said something. *Oh mon dieu!*" She couldn't stop the tears. This was not going at all like she'd planned. She passed Randy the card from her hotel. Managed to mumble some excuse about lunch while inviting him and his wife to dinner at 6.00pm with a voice that was falling apart. Without looking into his eyes again she turned and left, practically fled from him, down one street, blindly down another, away, away, down a narrow alley, to the left, to the right. To a dead end. She collapsed, on a pile of trash, and lay there, destroyed, in her new dress bought just for him. "*Oh mon dieu.* Oh Randy!"

11 Stung Again

"She's really here," said Randy to himself, as he approached his hotel. What a crazy coincidence. A sign? He wondered. He was always looking for signs in life, those events that say, "Yes, you are on the right path", or "No, run you've made a terrible mistake." The joy he felt at seeing her leaned him towards the first meaning. Meeting her was a good omen. Life had blessed him.

She had cried, actually cried with joy at seeing him! Did she still care so much, he wondered.

Theirs had been such a star-crossed relationship. She was married when they met, wanting only friendship. And he accepted that. But over the months they saw each other in Paris, in cafes and movie theaters, on long walks along the Seine, he realized he craved the look of her face, the sound of her voice, the touch of her hand.

He remembered them sitting in the dark, in a tiny theater in the Latin Quarter of Paris, watching a movie called "Little Voice." Like a teenager on a first date, he had tried to put his arm around her shoulders, only to have it shrugged off by her.

"No, Randy, someone might see," she whispered.

So he sat and watched the movie, feeling lonely, watched the part where this woman is gloriously happy, sure she has found love again, only to realize, devastatingly, that what she thought she had found was an illusion, that she was alone and would be alone the rest of her life.

When they left the theater, into the gray streets of old Paris, he suddenly burst into tears. The scene in the film had struck a chord in him, devastating him as well.

"What is it, Randy?" asked Julie, her face showing concern.

"I . . ." he tried to tell her, tried to stifle the emotion, but the sobs came louder. He turned, hid his face from her. But they were in a crowd. Everyone looking. He had no control. His heart had to empty itself.

Julie wrapped him in her arms, in the middle of the street. Told him that everything would be alright.

"I want you so much," he managed to say, to a married woman, in a foreign country, so far from home. "I am in love with you."

12 Home Sick

"You worked with her in Paris?" asks Fernanda, stretched out on the lumpy bed, her arms behind her head resting on an overstuffed pillow. The whirling blades of the ceiling fan wobble dangerously as Randy rubs Fernanda's bare feet.

"Yes, she was the manager on the Louvre project. I've told you about it, remember? When I lived in Paris. Before I came back to the states and searched you out."

"Vaguely," she said. "*Casi no.*" She raises up, swings her long legs over the edge of the bed, and gets up. Walks to the window and stands there, looking out over the river, at the few wooden boats. Vaguely wishes again that the boat she had fallen into had just kept on going.

"I don't like this place," she tells Randy. "I want to go home."

Randy does a double-take.

"You want to go home? We can't just go home. It's expensive to change the tickets. And anyway, I have to finish the project first. This is my career we are talking about."

"I want to…" she starts to say it again, but instead says. "I want to eat now."

She takes his hand and leads him to the door of their room.

Instead of going down to the river, they head out the back way from the hotel, through zagging narrow alley paths where kids with dirty faces look up from their games, where a policeman sits in a chair with a rifle from World War One across his lap. They pass tiny stall-like stores, finally reaching a wide street. They follow the street past sleeping dogs and marauding cows, past men and boys in rather drab western dress and women and girls in their colorful flowing saris. The dust on the road rises with each passing vehicle, car, truck, motorbike.

"We should have gone along the river," says Randy.

"There is no good place in this city," says Fernanda.

"Here," says Randy, "this restaurant looks promising." The building looks new and touristy, and they are the first for lunch.

Fernanda feels the drag of her internal clock telling her it is midnight at home, and time to sleep. She yawns. "OK."

As they walk in the restaurant to a table by the window,

Fernanda notices the air is freezing when directly below a vent, but walking between the vents she feels mugged by hot and humid air. Unnaturally hot and humid. Then freezing again. Nothing is normal in this city, she thinks, nothing in this city is as it should be.

"I want to go home," she whispers to herself as they sit down. A skinny teenage waiter comes with menus, two glasses and a bottle of water.

The menu offers vegetarian dishes only. Randy orders basmati rice and vegetables in a carrot cream sauce for the both of them.

"Strange for her to be here," says Fernanda.

"A miracle of a coincidence!" says Randy. "Think of the odds!"

"I think I'll be too sleepy to go to dinner. You go alone with her." She says, testing him.

"Of course not," Randy says. "If you aren't going, then I won't either."

"OK," says Fernanda. "But I'll try to make it because I know you want to go."

The food arrives, surprising Fernanda by how inviting it looks on the plate. The side dish of naan bread is hot with inflated pockets of goodness, reminding her of Mexican tortillas.

"The food is really good here," says Randy, after his first bite. Fernanda grunts, dipping her toasty warm naan into the creamy pink sauce.

13 We Give Our Lives To Our Companies

Randy spent early afternoon with the banks' computer staff, Neelu and Rakesh, in the cold computer room, reviewing the new system's manuals, backup procedures and automatic audit trail. Mr Tishwali popped his large head in the door once or twice, to check on them. Randy found his brain getting fuzzy around three o'clock and called a break. He stepped outside, walked the sidewalk, looking for a vendor of chocolate bars among the vendors of plastic toys, grapes and flowers.

"Coke?" asked Neelu.

He turned to see little Neelu standing right behind him, holding out to him an open bottle. Such friendly raccoon eyes.

He did not like coke but politely took the bottle she offered him. He even took a sip, before continuing on his walk.

"Your coming here is such a blessing," said Neelu. "I understand you volunteered?"

45

"I accepted the project, if that is what you mean," he told her.

"You are so important to the plan. To everything," she said, drinking her coke. "I didn't think Americans were religious, that is, the way we Hindus are. To give your life for our temple bank, this makes you truly a holy man who will recoup much in the next life."

Randy stopped short, trying to understand what she meant. "I am giving up a few days of my life for this project, yes. For the bank, as you say. But that is what we do when we work, no? Trade our work days for the weekends?"

Neelu frowned. Obviously they were having a cultural or verbal misunderstanding. He decided to drop the subject.

Before them, in the middle of the street, a brahma bull plodded along, interrupting traffic.

"Strange," said Randy, "how that bull is so tame. If such a bull were loose in Hot Springs everyone would be running inside."

"But why?" asked Julie.

"Bulls in general are aggressive animals. At least they are in the US."

"This animal is respected. No one will harm him. And he knows that."

They watched as he stopped, closed his eyes, and blocked out the external world.

"Shall we go back in?" said Randy. "I want to go over user account creation."

"Like giving birth to an entity," she said, "in the realm of the computer?"

"Sure," said Randy. "You can look at it like that."

"And every one is unique," she said.

You sure are, thought Randy, as they entered the dark alcove of the God Ganesh, where Neelu bent low and touched her fingers to the floor before him and transferred whatever it was that she received to the spot between her eyes.

14 An Offer Too Good

"All I know is I want to go home!" repeated Fernanda that evening as she sipped her coke and nibbled her naan in the open air restaurant on the rooftop of Julie's hotel. Below, as darkness fell on the river, boats of all sizes, with pilgrims and tourists, motored and rowed up and down, depositing a trail of flickering gold lights behind them.

"They look like tiny souls," said Julie, looking down on the river. "The candles. Flickering souls set adrift."

Randy looked at Fernanda then Julie.

"I think it's a good idea for you to leave, Fernanda," continued Julie, "if you really can't stand being here." She forced down a slug of beer, which she hated – but the hotel restaurant did not carry wine. She had enjoyed her basmati rice with cashew sauce – not spicy at all, which surprised her. She had enjoyed too hearing Randy's wife say she wanted to leave Varanasi; No, "enjoyed" is not the right word – she had been delighted to hear that Fernanda hated Varanasi. She looked at Randy and his wife. They did not even look like a couple, she decided. Randy too white and Fernanda too brown. You should go home, Julie thought, looking Fernanda directly in the eyes. You should go home and leave Randy to me!

Fernanda blinked. "I think it's incredible that Randy spotted you in the street," she said, under Julie's fixed stare.

Julie wondered what this Mexican woman was thinking. Was she internally critiquing Julie's thin Roman nose, her darting intelligent eyes, her high cheekbones, her refined yet fragile bearing. Julie knew her beauty was the opposite of Fernanda, a lusciously full-bodied, strong, natural woman who wore no makeup.

"Imagine my shock at running into an old colleague half way across the world!" Julie said, agreeing with Fernanda, looking to Randy. "I was floored!"

"The odds are infinitesimal," said Randy. "But life is like that. Always popping up with the impossible, to wake our unconscious up from its slumber. To let us know that the impossible is indeed possible."

"You always were a philosopher," said Julie, amused at the irony of how wrong he was. My little Randy. My innocent, gullible boy.

"I wish for the miracle of going home early," repeated

Fernanda, stretching her long strong arms.

"It's just too expensive," said Randy. "I can't change your ticket without practically buying another. And you don't really want to fly all that way alone. I know you."

"Hey!" said Julie, a plan forming as she spoke – she was good at that, after years of manipulating situations and personalities in French boardrooms, she was adept at scheming on her feet. "Flights within India are very cheap. In fact I'm leaving tomorrow for a wellness spa in Rishikesh, near the Himalayas. It's cool there and the spa treats you like a goddess. For $100 a week! The same spa in America would cost 2,000 dollars!"

"That sounds incredible," said Fernanda. This old colleague of her husband was impressively worldly. Flying all over by herself.

"Why don't you come with me?" proposed Julie, leaning towards Fernanda, holding out her hands. "We could fly out and back together."

"She couldn't," said Randy for her. He touched Fernanda's arm.

"Maybe I could," said Fernanda. "Me gusta la idea," she told Randy in Spanish, their personal language.

"I don't like it," said Randy. "You should just stay here."

Julie stretched down to her toes and back up again, saying

nonchalantly, "They say you lose ten pounds while gaining the softest complexion."

"I'm definitely going!" said Fernanda.

"No," said Randy. "It's best if you stay with me until I finish the project."

"You just don't want to be alone," said Fernanda. "You're being selfish."

Chaotic music from downriver rose up to them on their perch atop Varanasi. A loud speaker squawked and a man began to speak.

"Listen," said Julie. "They are beginning the Aarti prayer ceremony. A festive event they do every night on the ghats. You must see one before you leave."

"I'm leaving tomorrow," said Fernanda. "With you. Randy can enjoy all the ceremony and bull shit here in Varanasi by himself." She got up. Randy stood too.

"You're serious?" said Julie. "You want to come with me to Rishikesh?"

"Yes."

"Great. I can make the arrangements in the morning. I'll need your passport, though."

"Randy?"

Randy fished out her passport from his back pocket. "I think it's a bad idea," he mumbled as they told Julie goodnight and headed down the painted concrete steps to catch a tuktuk back to their hotel at the Meer Ghat. "Not a good idea," he repeated.

Julie watched them disappear down the steps, waving after them. She returned to her place at the table, looked down on the holy river. She felt both excited and tranquil. How quickly luck can change in your favor! How wonderful that Fernanda wanted to leave Varanasi as much as Julie wanted her to go.

Now if she could only convince Fernanda to go to Rishikesh by herself. For of course Julie'd bought no ticket nor had any spa reservation. Oh sure she'd researched spas in Rishikesh, with an eye to going there if Randy did not show or had got all fat or disfigured in an auto accident. A lot can happen in two years – in her case a divorce, in his a marriage. But luckily he had neither gotten fat nor been horribly disfigured. He was still the man she had fallen for in Paris. So her question was, how could she get Fernanda to go alone to Rishikesh, and leave Randy all to herself?

Julie sat at the table for some time, looking down on the Ganges with its sprinkle of failing candles, with its musical chants of a people praying to a different god. Maybe to her god, but with a different name. A different form. Julie sat and thought, and finally, as the music died and the people and their gods nodded off, Julie came up with another plan.

15 Like Burned Popcorn

Randy dropped Fernanda at the hotel. Told her he felt like a walk.

"You're mad at me," said Fernanda. "Because I want to leave."

"No. I now think you should go. I want you to do what you want."

"I won't go. I'll stay," said Fernanda.

"No, really. I want you to go to that spa. I think you will enjoy that more than staying here with me. I just want to stretch my legs before I hit the sack. I won't be long." And he left.

He lied. He was angry, especially at that meddling Julie. He hoped the walk would help him settle down. Why was Julie here, anyway, he wondered? Why had fate or God or whoever brought her back into his life, in all places, here, in Varanasi? Was it because, as they said, this was a holy place, a place for miracles? Was her return into his life really some act of God? Were they meant to be together after all? Thoughts such as these rambled round his head as he made his way along the different levels and awkwardly joined steps of the ghats.

He had wanted her once, was he afraid of wanting her again?

In the light of a small bonfire at water's edge, he noticed an older gent in what looked like a wetsuit, loading scuba air bottles under a seat in a wide row boat. This was of particular interest to Randy because he had learned to scuba the year before on his honeymoon on the big island of Hawaii.

"You can scuba in the Ganges?"

The cleanshaven man turned kind eyes on Randy. "Not unless it is your duty," he said. "Do you scuba?"

"Yes," said Randy.

"Good, I need a helper. You can follow your dharma and accompany me tomorrow. Sunrise. Meet me here at the boat."

"My dharma? I have work to do tomorrow. Well, at 10.00 am anyway."

"Oh that's plenty of time to do what must be done. My name is Raj." He held out his hand and Randy felt the strong grip. "You must not miss this chance to earn merit, for your next life."

"I'm Randy. My next life?" Reincarnation was not something Randy often worried about. "I'm a bit too busy in this life to worry about the next one."

"Listen. Listen," the old man said, seemingly anxious to keep Randy's attention. "I am the official keeper of the carrion eaters in the river Ganga. The great snapping turtles. Since 1984 when I released them. I suggest that you help me tag them."

"Snapping turtles?"

"Sit. Sit." He padded the ghat step. "Maybe after you hear my story you will be more obliged to help?"

Randy sat next to the man on the steps next to the small bonfire, which flared occasionally sending incredible heat upon them, for a second, then the cool night breeze took over again.

"For thousands of years the dead have gone into the Ganga, or the Ganges river as you westerner's call it, here at the Manikarnika Ghat," Raj told Randy. "Most are burned to ashes and tossed in the river, but holy men, lepers, pregnant women, and children under twelve, when they die, they are tied to those flat stones over there and taken out in the river and dumped to the bottom. Like Christians and Muslims dump their people in the ground to rot. Imagine the pile of corpses, though, after a thousand years of such dumping! Rotting bodies polluting the river, bloating and breaking apart, floating to the surface, scaring the bathers!"

The bonfire popped. Randy looked into the fire and noticed, "Oh my gosh, a body."

An awkward bare blackened leg stuck out of the flames, the foot slowly twisting downward as if the body in the fire was rolling over.

"He is low caste," said Raj. "In the section higher up is the middle caste."

Randy looked and saw more fires there.

"And up on top are the high caste, the Brahmins – you know, teachers, technicians, lawyers, doctors."

"The smell is strange," said Randy. "Bad. Like burned popcorn."

"Relatives and friends butter their dead, so they will burn quickly. The corpses are only allowed to burn for three hours, before what is left is dumped in the river," said Raj, rubbing his nose. "So, back to the problem of the floating dead – in the early eighties a group of scientists like me got together and came up with a pretty good, though not perfect, solution. We seeded the river with specially trained snapping turtles. Turtles that we raised only on carrion. On dead flesh. So their natural feeding place would be the middle of the river, would be the rotting flesh of the innocent dead."

Randy swallowed. Looked out at the current. Tried to imagine a graveyard at the bottom of the river.

Raj rose slowly to his feet. "So you will come tomorrow? And help with the turtles? I need to tag them, and do a census while I am in the river this week."

Randy hesitated. The idea scared him and excited him at the same time. "Sure. I'd love to help."

"This isn't Tahiti," said Raj. "The water can be murky as curry."

"I've dived murky," said Randy. "And I like curry. If not too spicy." They shook hands and Raj left Randy sitting on the warm step, musing about the dive the next day to the underwater cemetery. He'd forgotten all about his woman trouble. Forgotten all about how his heart had been broken by Julie in Paris, and how Fernanda wanted to abandon him once again.

The bonfire popped and Randy turned to look once again. This time he made out a head in the fire, a bald head with a flaming red ribbon on top. The body shifted, the head turned. Randy looked into eyes he recognized, suffering eyes in that blackened face. This burning man was the holy, crippled man he'd seen that morning at The First Ganesh Bank of Varanasi, he was sure of it, the man with the walking stick who withdrew an impossible amount of rupees. This man he'd seen, this man he saw now, was lying in a bonfire, still alive! The man was alive!

Randy jumped and started to reach into the wall of heat, to pull the man free, but the eyes told him No, please, let me go.

Randy stood inches from the unbearable heat, inches from a body being consumed with fire. The skin on his partially outstretched hand felt it would explode from the heat. He stood immobile, watching as the black flesh on the skull peeled away and the eyes melted and the skull with now empty sockets crumpled and turned to ash.

16 Turtles All The Way Down

"Your imagination, young Randy?" suggested Raj, the next morning, as they put on wet suits in an unlocked storage room carved into the wide stairs next to the cremation ghat. "Death up close can play havoc with a human mind that refuses to admit one day it will cease to be."

A smoke-like fog spread tendrils over the river, up the steps of the ghat, threatening to swallow the city and all its inhabitants.

"Perhaps," Randy admitted, struggling to squeeze into the too tight rubber suit. Still the memory of those eyes staring at him from the fire, eyes that begged to be let go, left him with a sense of foreboding. That and the fact that Fernanda was leaving in an hour, leaving him alone to finish the bank project in Varanasi, while she flew off with Julie to a health spa in picturesque Rishikesh.

"Something bad's going to happen," said Randy aloud.

"No," said Raj, "you will see. With one person it is quite

difficult to hold a 3', 100lb turtle in place to read its existing tag or staple on a new one. But with two working as a team, you'll see, it will be most entertaining!"

They placed their tanks of air into their BC vests, checked the pressure in the tanks, Randy careful to point the glass cover of the gauge away from his face when he turned on the air, as a blown gauge cover under 1300 psi was a good way to lose an eye. Raj helped Randy zip up the last few inches of the suit, and they strapped on the vests with the tanks. Randy had forgotten how heavy it all was, as he leaned forward and walked stiff legged down the steps with his flippers and mask in hand, walked down to the row boat tied at the bottom of the ghat.

As Raj rowed 75 yards offshore, he told Randy the story of how a highly educated man from Great Britain came to India in colonial times and asked a poor uneducated Hindu woman about the Hindu myth that says that the world sits atop the back of a giant turtle.

"So the world sits atop a turtle?" asked the educated Brit sitting in a high chair.

"Yes," replied the woman, squatting on the ground before him.

"And what is the turtle standing on?" asked the highly

educated man, sure he had the uneducated woman with his impeccable logic.

"Why, another turtle, of course," replied the woman, as if stating the obvious.

"And what is that turtle standing on?" the educated man asked, pushing home his point.

"Turtles," replied the old woman, exasperated with how thick this foreigner was. "It's turtles all the way down."

Randy laughed. Despite the frightening night he'd had, despite the knowledge that he would soon be alone in India, despite the fog of the morning swallowing the ghats, swallowing their boat as they lay anchor and prepared to drop overboard into the Ganges' graveyard of innocents, despite all this he felt his spirits elevated by Raj's story. The world did not have to make sense. The world made its own sense. Turtles all the way down.

They caught their first one halfway to the bottom — two foot long, cruising by them with all the time in the world. Randy held on as he'd been told, to the front legs, from behind, stalling the beast as best he could from swimming, while avoiding the rock hard jaws. Raj pulled out his staple gun and shot a numeric ID tag into the thick webbed skin of its left front flipper. Randy released the turtle and it quickly swam out of sight.

The million bodies, old bones mostly, that had been dropped into this spot in the Ganges for more than a thousand years formed a small mountain that peaked some 30' to 50' below the surface, the real earth bottom being much deeper. Visibility was bad enough that Raj used a spot. The piles and piles of human bones, coming in and out of Raj's light, reminded Randy of the catacombs of Paris, a place Julie took him to, a place Julie loved – where the bones of six million poor French are stacked in cold damp caves under the wide, lovely boulevards. Julie, now that he thought about it, often brought to mind dark, heavy imaginings, even the promise of death, whereas Fernanda brought to his mind brightness and the promise of life.

Raj and Randy swam up the wall of the manmade underwater mountain of bodies, to a spread of corpses whose freshly torn ghostly flesh waved in the current like white grass. Luckily Randy could not see them all at once, the water was too murky for that, instead the dead paraded by him intimately as he kicked alongside Raj, the horror of an eyeless boy of ten, an open mouthed woman pregnant and bloated with a dead baby inside never to be born except from rot or the feeding of the turtles.

Randy knew he should feel terror at such a sight, but instead the view, this underwater horror show, intrigued him. There could be no place like this anywhere else in the world. And fate had allowed him to experience it. And to see them.

The turtles. There were scores of them here. Hundreds, then thousands of the beasts, it seemed, were caught in the spotlight. Like a herd of round cows grazing. The only sound the gurgle of bubbles releasing, with each breath, from Raj and Randy's regulators.

They spent the next hour recording tags, Raj writing with a special waterproof pen on oiled paper, and stamping untagged animals, Randy suffering a couple of strong bites, thankful for the thick rubber gloves Raj had provided, which both protected him and allowed him to slip his gripped hand from their jaws.

So many turtles, spread across this field of decay, turtles on bodies, turtles on turtles, turtles all the way down.

Raj's masked face popped up before Randy, and Randy was taken aback by the bloodless look of that face. The man looked ghastly. Like the face of a dead man. Randy knew this was the result of the depths filtering out the color red. Still, the thought struck him that a dead man was showing him the underwater cemetery, maybe taking him to his own underwater grave?

Raj signed with his hands to Randy, 'How much air left?'

Randy checked his gauge and flashed the number four for 400 psi.

Raj pointed up – time to go. His body revolved in slow motion, rising now, in front of Randy. Randy followed his flippers. They somehow found the anchor line and followed it up, slowly, stopping occasionally, never rising faster than their bubbles, allowing their bodies time to equalize. They had been down to as much as two atmospheres of pressure – going down that far it's your ears to worry about – you can blow out your eardrums if you go down too fast; but come up too fast and it's both the air in your lungs and the nitrogen in your tissue to worry about. The air can explode your lungs and the nitrogen, if you decompress too quickly, will bubble and catch in all the hurtful places of your body and if it doesn't kill you it will make you wish it had.

They broke surface. Raj climbed in the boat first, then helped Randy who had some difficulty. Already a few tourist boats cruised the river. Already a body strapped to a tombstone was being rowed in their direction from the cremation ghat. A dead holy man by the look of him, as the boat passed. Turtle bait.

"I've got to rush to the First Ganesh Bank," said Randy, once they reached shore and he realized the time. He quickly dried off and dressed in the storage room. "Would you like me to come again tomorrow?"

"Tomorrow is the day before Hindu holiday," said Raj. "I have a long drive home, so I am leaving in the morning. I won't be back until Monday."

"Oh," said Randy. "Then Monday morning?"

"Yes please, young Randy. I would be most obliged if you could help again Monday morning. Sunrise. Until then." And he bowed his goodbye.

17 How They Met

Julie and Fernanda sat together on the flight to Delhi, where they were to catch a connecting flight to Dehradun, the closest airport to Rishikesh in the rugged north. Julie breathed easy now after the rush that morning to make ashram reservations with the help of the hotel manager. Things will work out, she told herself. Will work out for the best.

"So how did you and Randy meet?" Julie asked, trying to make polite conversation with her adversary.

"When I was 17, working in a whorehouse in Nuevo Laredo, Mexico," said Fernanda. She laughed at the look on Julie's face.

"Bueno, it's not as bad as it sounds," she explained, throwing back her hair. "I played trumpet in my father's mariachi band. Since I was little. He booked us to play that night in a sex club where Randy and Randy's friend Chance happened to visit."

Julie's interest was piqued by this unexpected tale. Randy visiting a sex club? That seemed so out of character.

"Somehow Chance got arrested," continued Fernanda, "for assaulting one of the girls in the show, the girl who does, you know, with a mule, leaving Randy with no way home, so I let him sleep on my porch until we could get Chance from jail and then Randy kissed me and promised to take me to America which he did but then the plan went wrong and *entonces* I ended up with Chance on a quartz mine in Arkansas for years, *anos*, until Chance cheated on me and then Randy came back into my life and we married."

Fernanda leaned back and caught her breath.

Julie sat wide-eyed.

"Wow," she said finally. "*C'est beaucoup!* That's a lot to take in. So you two didn't meet recently, but many years ago?" Julie had thought that she had met Randy first, before Fernanda had, and so had dibs, so to speak, but now she realized that wasn't necessarily the case.

"Yes, when we were both young. Too young then, I think," said Fernanda. "And how were you two met?"

Normally Julie would have told a simple lie, that they were introduced in some boring hallway while working on the same project in Paris a couple of years ago, but after Fernanda's romantic tale, she felt obliged to mix in a bit of the truth.

"We had seen each other in the offices of the Louvre, me managing a project for the museum and Randy assisting on that project as an IBM consultant. But we had never talked until we met accidentally one evening in Le Danton, a brasserie next to the Odeon metro stop. Randy had just seen an Ingmar Bergman film, Cries and Whispers, and started talking to me about it, out of the blue. We had that in common, a love of great cinema. We found too we shared a love of Paris."

Fernanda frowned, obviously uneasy with that pronouncement. "You were married?" she asked.

"I was," said Julie. "Back then. That's one reason I took this vacation. To get over my recent divorce."

"I'm sorry," said Fernanda, "so now you are single?"

"I am getting over the divorce," she told her, "over those terrible feelings of failure. But that was one reason I really couldn't show Randy around Paris much, back then when we worked together. My husband was just too jealous." She paused, took a sip of water. "Randy is a likable guy. I wished him the best when he left . . . France." And she forced herself to say, "And I am so glad he found someone like you to marry."

Julie noticed how Fernanda relaxed. She had sold her on her innocence.

"So strange, though," said Fernanda, "that an old colleague

69

like you would appear in Varanasi the same week we arrive."

Fernanda visited a book store at the terminal in Delhi while Julie found a place to dial out and read her email. In the bookstore she perused books about Indian culture, famous Indian people and something called Kamasutra. The pictures on the cover of a large Kamasutra book showed statues of people embracing, but between the covers, inside the book, the pictures were so explicit and acrobatic that Fernanda felt the blood rising to her face.

"Oh, *c'est pas vrai!*" Julie exclaimed, coming up suddenly on Fernanda, who instinctively dropped the book to the floor. There it lay, open to a naked couple twisting around and inside each other. Fernanda grabbed up the book and put it back on the shelf, while Julie pointed out to Fernanda an email she'd received from her company. Fernanda tried to read the tiny text but Julie slammed the case closed in disgust. "Can you believe that bastard? He knows I am in eastern India so he asks me to go to Khajuraho to a UNESCO meeting there. Apparently my company is involved with setting up legal contracts and coordinating the effort to establish the temples there as a world heritage site. Can you believe this? Just when I am off to a week of princess spa treatment, they want me to fly to a boring meeting!"

"Your boss wants you to go now? Can't you refuse?" asked Fernanda, disquieted with the thought of traveling on alone. She wondered if she should return as well.

"Working for a French company," said Julie, "I've discovered you can argue all you want but in the end you do what your manager asks or you get transferred to a powerless position filing others' papers."

"But you're on vacation!" cried Fernanda.

"Yes, but work comes first." She walked Fernanda to her gate, with Fernanda practically dragging her feet, protesting, "But. Maybe I shouldn't. If you can't go."

"No I insist," said Julie. "Go for my benefit! Enjoy yourself for me!"

The boarding call for their flight to Dehradun sounded. A line formed, with Julie and Fernanda at the rear. Julie continued to reassure Fernanda, even took her boarding pass and handed it to the airline clerk, who checked it and gave it back to Fernanda.

"Remember girl, everything is arranged. There will be a driver at the airport with our names on a plaque. He will get you safely to the health spa. Then back to the airport in a week."

"But," said Fernanda one last time.

"Please, Fernanda. I want this for you. You deserve it. Go, please, for me!" She kissed Fernanda on both cheeks and gently pushed her towards the ramp. Fernanda shrugged and walked down the boarding ramp, digging in her purse for her calming valerian root capsules.

"Bon voyage!"

18 Variables And Constants, People And Their Gods

After lunch Randy hovered over his two young students, Neelu, the girl with the underbite and Rakesh, a good looking twenty something Indian lad with a crewcut, the Ganesh Bank's computer support staff, as they typed in their first computer programs. Randy had lectured for an hour on the basics of Basic, the stored procedure language of the bank's new database called UniVerse, and now he had them applying a bit of what he had taught.

The morning had gone reasonably well despite the fact Fernanda had left with Julie for a health spa in Rishikesh: first his successful dive with biologist Raj to the turtle feeding grounds, then the successful launch of the bank's new computer system. Randy had supervised all transactions made by the tellers, and confirmed that all updates were happening as they should. There would be no more holes for money to disappear into. The bank had been brought up to the latest technology. And after a phone conversation between Randy, Mr Tishwali and the Deposit Insurance and Credit Guarantee

Corporation of India representative, all the banks accounts were now federally insured.

Mr Tishwali had a lunch of vegetables and rice brought in for the computer staff, after which Randy started their computer coding instruction.

They were deep into their first program, a simple report, when the door to the computer room opened, breaking their concentration. In came Mr Tishwali, the brain behind the bank management according to what Neelu had told him at lunch. Next to Mr Tishwali strode a thin man in orange holy robes. The holy man had a crooked nose, severe eyes, and long reddish hair. His face and bare arms were covered with gray-white ash, giving him a ghostly pallor.

"My partner, Asha" said Mr Tishwali. "This is Mr Randy from IBM." Randy shook hands with the ash faced man and though his name was Asha not Ash, Randy would always think of him as Ash.

"So tell me what you've learned so far," Mr Tishwali said to Neelu.

She moved her underbite jaw left and right, as if chewing a bone, and spoke, "Well, we learned about program constants who are like the Gods in our world, always with the value they are meant to have. And we learned about variables who in our world are like hearts that take on different emotions, but variables are more logical. And lastly we learned do-until program loops which in our world can be thought of as reincarnation, where we loop again and again building karma until we reach Nirvana."

Randy laughed. "Well, there is the possibility of an endless loop. But we don't like those in programming."

"Nor in life," said Asha in a voice that cracked dryly. Randy caught his smell then, and almost gagged. He wondered how the others ignored it. The man reeked.

Trying his best to ignore the offensive odor, Randy thanked Neelu for her presentation. The teacher in Randy was proud of Neelu. He hadn't made any of Neelu's points when lecturing the past hour, but as Neelu spoke he understood that, like all of us when we learn something new, she had to tie these programming concepts to her own notions of how the world works.

"Outstanding," said Mr Tishwali, blaring his words as usual. He turned to Randy, his eyes glistening. "Now all this computer knowledge you are sharing doesn't put in jeopardy the security of the system?"

"Oh, no," said Randy, addressing Mr Tishwali and Asha with his best IBM demeanor. "I am teaching them the basics so they can eventually write reports or change existing ones. They won't be able to hack the system."

"But someone like you could?" asked Mr Tishwali. "Someone

like you could move money into fictitious accounts, could hide transactions? Could rob us blind?"

"Well, I suppose I could do that, but not without leaving a trail," said Randy, a bit hurt by such talk. "That's the beauty of this new system – encrypted, offsite auditing. Anyway, before I leave I will have Neelu delete my account."

"Still the idea troubles me," said Mr Tishwali. "Perhaps I will have you do a test before you leave." He looked to Asha, who nodded, and turned back to Randy. "Anyway, I told the tellers to do whatever you say while you are here, without bothering me for permission. I do have complete faith in you, Mr Randy."

Asha stared at Randy, who found the stare of such a severe holy man disquieting.

"But all of that is not why I came in. Asha and I would like to invite you all to a celebration at my house this evening. We are going to feast and give thanks to Ganesh for the successful launch of the new system." He handed Randy a card with his address. "Any taxi or tuktuk can get you there."

At four the bank shut its doors, and the next half hour they spent running pre-conciliations, a task that used to take 2 hours but now was done in a matter of minutes. When all looked right for the nightly run, Randy left the building.

Right into the arms of Julie. She threw herself around him, squeezing him with all her might.

"So wonderful, so wonderful, so wonderful to see you again!" she said, acting so unlike herself – acting like a 3 year old.

"But aren't you . . . where is Fernanda?" He managed to get one of her arms from around his neck.

"Fernanda is at the health spa in Rishikesh. At the ashram," said Julie. "I had to fly back. I was ordered by my boss to return for a business meeting. In Khajuraho. Not far."

"Fernanda isn't with you? She went alone?"

"Don't worry, Randy, she's fine. You can call her later."

She was still partially wrapped around him when Mr Tishwali and Asha came outside the bank.

"Oh excellent, Mr Randy. Your wife. You must bring her to the festivities tonight as well!"

"Oh she's not . . ." he started to say, but already Mr Tishwali and his partner had merged into the swell of afternoon shoppers.

"Sounds like we have a date?" said Julie, finally releasing him. She stood back and he was amazed how lively she looked, how young, how desirable. Not dark-spirited at all.

Randy hesitated. "Sure," he said finally. "Why not? We're old friends. But now I have to go to the hotel and call Fernanda."

"That's fine," said Julie. "I'll go with you. We can walk along the ghats. I want to catch up on what you've done these past years, besides getting married."

19 Harmony Of The Mind And Body

Fernanda walks through a sparkling hall in the immaculate white health spa that sits on a green hill overlooking the Ganges river, overlooked itself by the snowcapped peaks of the Himalayas. Her high heels echo loudly, announcing her arrival.

A barefoot girl walks before her, she does not speak but gestures. Fernanda follows her into a sparsely furnished room where a small table sits next to a mat on the concrete floor. Fernanda puts down her bag, thinking, What is this? My prison cell?

A hand touches her shoulder. She turns and it is not the girl but a barefoot man in a white gown. His long black hair is pulled back, his expression is serene. His eyes hypnotic.

"Welcome to Harmony House," he tells her. "I am Win, your teacher."

"My teacher?" asks Fernanda. "I thought this was a health spa."

"Yes but of course there is no physical health without mental and spiritual health. It is my job to teach you all three. If you are settled, then let's begin with a tour."

She follows him about the place, noticing the blank walls, the spotless floors, the practically unfurnished rooms. She comments on the lack of "things."

"This is lesson one," Win tells her. "You must learn to unclutter your life, as we have uncluttered Harmony House. I will teach you how to unclutter your body of unneeded, harmful fat, your mind of unuseful thoughts and your soul of wasteful energy."

Speaking of energy, the man practically radiates the stuff. An attractive energy. He is a charming, charmful man.

"Can we visit the town?" asks Fernanda.

"After dinner I will escort you," says Win.

Dinner is a portion of peas and rice that could fit in a girl's palm. Fernanda cleans her small plate, leaves the table, and goes to her room still hungry. A knock. She opens and Win is there.

"Are you ready for our walk?" he asks, his eyes sparkling he is in such good health. He is a walking advertisement for Harmony House, thinks Fernanda.

They cross the bridge over the Ganges, walking towards town, Fernanda hungry enough to take a bite from Win's perfectly smooth neck.

They walk in silence, Win typically only speaking when spoken to, Fernanda busy trying to ignore the fried food stands in the narrow streets of Rishikesh. Oh but they look good, the breaded potato pies and the sweet twisty funnel-cake-like pastries.

As if reading her mind, Win stops and asks a vendor for an order of twisties. "Dessert," he says, offering the goodies to Fernanda.

"Oh I shouldn't," she says, grabbing hold of one end and dropping the warm sweet pastry into her mouth.

"No you shouldn't," he says, laughing. "But tonight, your first night, all is allowed."

They walk the opposite bank of the river from Harmony House, where holy men have pitched tents. Win tries to steer Fernanda away, but she is naturally drawn to the crowd of tourists and pilgrims in front of the tents.

She pushes her way to the front of the crowd, in front of the middle-aged, middle class men and women, mostly Indian in Indian dress, a few westerners. Win follows close behind her.

At first she doesn't understand what she is seeing. A holy man, naked from the waist down, is wearing a rod through his penis. No – she realizes as he gives the rod another crank – he is stretching his penis around the rod like you'd wind up a long hose. He is stretching his part beyond belief.

She reaches a hand back to Win, to steady herself. "A freak show?" she asks him.

"Fakirs," says Win. "They learn control of their bodies, control over pain. The Gods bless them with power for giving up the pleasures of life."

"Is this what you teach?" asks Fernanda.

"This is a tributary of what I teach," says Win. "Since we are already here, come, follow me. I will show you one of my former students."

They walk over stones to a red tent where another small group of tourists and pilgrims stand. This time Win pushes their way to the front of the crowd. The homey smell of snow and wild goats wafts on the breeze rolling down from the mountains.

Sitting crosslegged before them in the center of the red tent a holy man wearing only ash and a head scarf is staring at his penis.

What is it with all these naked men!

Fernanda watches in shock as the penis grows from peanut size to a good foot-long cucumber. He raises his eyes and meets Fernanda's stare, unashamed, almost proud. Someone in the crowd claps. The holy man touches a finger to his lips for silence. Then he touches his finger to the red spot between his eyes, and the penis begins to shrink back to its quiescent state. Fernanda frowns, starts to walk, but Win tells her, "Wait."

The holy man looks down and touches the red dot between his eyes again, and again his part comes alive, without him touching it, standing up straight in a matter of seconds.

The crowd applauds and puts a few rupees in the basket at his feet.

"Control," says Win as they cross the bridge back to Harmony House. "This is what I can teach you. Control over your breathing, your eating, over your heartbeat, over loneliness, over depression. Over the state of being human. And, yes, if you wish, I can even teach you control of your sex."

Fernanda feels her heart skip a beat. She is over her head. Why did she let Randy bring her to India? Why did she let Julie talk her into coming to Rishikesh, only to abandon her? Fernanda's heart races, the top of her head feels effervescent. Panic strikes her in the middle of the bridge as she realizes she is not in control of her life.

"Help me," she says, falling against Win.

"I will," he promises.

Down on the smooth boulders of the river bank, listening to the rumors of the river as it rushes down from high mountain, a girl in ancient dress watches the couple on the bridge and shakes her head. "No, this will not do," she says to herself. "This will not do at all."

20 The Purpose Of Life Is To Invent One

Randy and Julie sat at Mr Tishwali's large wood dining table with several of the staff from the First Ganesh Bank of Varanasi, with Neelu and Rakesh and a couple of clerks and tellers. They'd just finished off the feast in Ganesh's honor, a wonderful meal of buttered naan and basmati rice with raisins and cashews, and a sweet tomato sauce with vegetables. They drank lassi, a non-alcoholic yogurt drink, toasting themselves, the Gods and IBM.

At the table Randy started to explain that Julie was an old friend and not his wife, but before he could begin he was interrupted with talk of the incident of the beggar man at the bank who withdrew such a large sum the other day.

"You see," explained Mr Tishwali. "Asha devised a plan a year ago to have poor holy men come to the bank every once in a while, come to the bank and withdraw huge sums from fake accounts he'd set up for them. For the show of it. To get people talking – did you see, even holy men keep their cash at Ganesh Bank! And see what luck they have with their savings!"

Asha looked down.

"And the plan worked great, with each holy man secretly returning the money to us. Only this last time, that morning you arrived Mr Randy, the holy man disappeared with the cash! So much for free advertising! So much for supposed holy men!"

"Perhaps he didn't run off," said Randy. "Perhaps he was robbed and killed."

Everyone turned and looked at Randy.

"I saw him," continued Randy. "That same night. I saw him burning at the Manikarnika Ghat."

That silenced everyone. What was Randy talking about?

"Well that doesn't make any sense," said the young clerk Rakesh. "Holy men aren't burned when they die."

"I don't think he was dead," said Randy. "I think he was burned alive!"

That got Asha and Mr Tishwali talking rapidly in Hindi. The other guests listened intently.

Julie leaned over and whispered to Randy, "Why didn't you go to the police?"

"I wasn't sure," he whispered back. He spoke aloud for all to hear. "I am not sure he was alive. Maybe it was my imagination. I can't even be sure it was the same man."

That calmed the scene a bit. Still Randy felt bad about darkening the mood. Now was not the time to start explaining about his non-wife either. He decided to change the subject entirely. "So tell me how you two happened to open a bank," he asked of Mr Tishwali and Asha.

Mr Tishwali's wide shoulders relaxed. He called to his wife to clear the table.

"We grew up together. Our folks did not have the money to raise us, so they gave us over to the monks," said Mr Tishwali. His wife came in from the kitchen with a bowl of green grapes and small bananas.

"I did not like living in a monastery, begging with the others for food. I wanted to earn a living, to stand on my own two feet. So when Asha told me he was running away, to work at the crematorium, I begged for him to take me. I was ten and he was twelve. The night manager at the crematorium knew we were not untouchables, but we told him we would work for two meals a day only. So he performed a ceremony to make us untouchables, and we went to work for him at night, sifting the ashes of the dead for anything of value, while throwing leftovers into the river."

He paused, wiped his mouth on a napkin.

"Those were hard times. But kids adapt, you know? We worked at night and slept in cubby holes of the ghats during the day. And slowly we learned about money, about how the keepers of money, the bankers, were like gods to the poor. And we learned what money could buy and how to make money ourselves, either touting tourists on the ghats to certain boatmen and hotels, or from our work, where, although we were only paid with food, we discovered that Aghori sadhus would pay hundreds of rupees for good drinking skulls for their taboo-breaking ceremonies. So we stole the heads from bodies in the lower fires, from the burning corpses of the poor and disregarded. We used sharp sticks and sand to clean the skulls, and soap we stole from the women washing clothes on stones in the river." Mr Tishwali wiped his watery eyes. Winked a wet eye at Randy. "Then one night, instead of turning over the five gold teeth I'd sifted from the hot ashes, instead of giving them to the night manager, I decided to keep them for myself. I placed the teeth in my own mouth. Burning hot they were. Yet I learned to talk that night, even smile, with my gums full of hot gold teeth. And my plan worked. I got away with it. So every night, opportunity allowing, I repeated my thievery, hiding half of my findings, then after work hoarding them in a slot behind my sleeping hole in the steps of the Ganges. I did this for years, not even telling Asha, who spent more and more of his free time with the Aghori's, smoking ganji and learning spiritual things that did not interest me."

"He told me nothing for years," said Asha. "About his thefts. For he did not want to risk getting me burned alive as well, if he were caught by the night manager with a mouthful of gold." Asha looked fondly at his friend. "Until one night, I must have been about 17, one night after work he says to me, I wonder how much to buy that abandoned temple where the dogs sleep? I think it would make a good bank."

"Yes," said Mr Tishwali, "I remember as if it were yesterday. And you said, what a crazy question. What money do we have that we could open a bank? And in a temple, no less? So I open my mouth, reach inside, and pull out a gold ring with a diamond the size of a cat's eye."

"You should have seen it," said Asha. "Sparkling with the promise of a new life. But still I told him, even that is not enough. That's when he told me to hold on, and he took out his full treasure from his little cubby-hole hiding place, and laid it before me. I laughed. You are a great thief, I told him. I will ask my Aghori elders to help us buy the temple and we shall start our bank as you wish. A bank for the people. In honor of Ganesh. And that's how all this came about. That's what brought you here. Tishwali's brazen thievery."

Mr Tishwali rose from his place, took a kind of bow. "Ah but please don't repeat this story." He winked again. "Reputation to upkeep, and all that." He turned his wide body and headed to the stairs.

"Let's retire to the roof," he said. As Randy followed the

heavyset man, along with the others, single file, to the roof, he wondered why Mr Tishwali dared to confess all this to him. How could he be so sure that Randy would never tell another soul? Once on the roof, he settled on a couch under the stars.

"I bring smoke!" said Asha, appearing at the top of the stairs carrying an enormous chillum pipe. He lit the pipe with what he claimed to be the eternal flame from the Manikarnika Ghat. The same flame that lit up the dead, the flame that could get you to Nirvana. He took a drag from the oversized pipe, his face with that long crooked nose and severe eyes enveloped in a cloud of thick swirling smoke. He passed the pipe on to little Neelu who took a measured draw. Eventually the pipe found its way to Randy. He held the warm pipe, not sure what to do. The smoke had that bitter sweet smell he recognized from his teenage years, when his crazy friend Chance used to smoke pot in the car with him at the Gemini Drive-in Theater.

Asha motioned for Randy to try it. "To better discourse with God," he said.

So Randy did, and passed the pipe to Julie. She took a pull and coughed. Round and round the pipe went, all but Mr Tishwali sharing the smoke.

Powerful stuff, thought Randy. Or did he just say that aloud?

Asha stood and began to explain that man's true purpose was to sacrifice to the Gods.

Randy begged to differ, arguing that man's purpose for being was to learn enough to create the universe.

"The universe that's already created?" puzzled Rakesh, the other I.T. person to whom Randy was teaching program logic.

Randy nodded. "That is the beauty of it."

Randy stood, he couldn't remember why, then tripped and hit his knee hard on the concrete roof. And didn't feel a thing. He put his hand down to get to his feet, but his hand couldn't tell where lay the concrete floor.

"Strong stuff," he said aloud, or did he just think it? Asha helped him to his feet. "Where was I going?"

"Where are any of us going, after this short illusion of life?" said Asha, laughing, his smell oozing from him as a brownish purple gas. Randy tried to wave it away as Asha guided him back to the couch next to Julie.

"How long have you two been married?" asked Neelu, wiggling her nose. Julie looked to Randy to respond, but he couldn't remember the question. His mind was too flooded with the closeness of Julie. Her body. Her face. She was easily the most desirable woman in Varanasi.

He tried to tell her so but only gibberish came out. Julie puzzled a moment, then replied for him, "Two years now."

She snuggled up to Randy. Touched his face which felt hot. She kissed him and he kissed her back, his wife, wasn't she? Such pretty eyes, bloodshot or not.

And that's the last thing he remembered of the night's events. He woke naked next to Julie in her bed at the Grand Palace Hotel. A rooster crowed. Morning already.

"I knew something bad would happen if she left. I knew it!" he told himself, thinking of Fernanda. He slipped carefully out of bed, trying not to wake Julie. With an eye on her naked back he searched the floor for his underwear.

21 The Gods' Dilemma

"What is Desire but the mask of procreation?" asked Lord Hanuman, the monkey God, high atop the Anapurna Range. His featherweight steps left no prints on the snow's crust.

"Desire desecrates all things Holy," countered Kali behind him, in woman form, caressing a dead cat. "I like that."

In the distance, they could just make out the pacing form of Shiva, the Auspicious One, patron God of yoga and the arts. They both bowed to him; he did not bow back.

"He worries over his precious Ganga, his river of life," said Kali. "It swallows all. It will swallow this Love."

"I don't know," said Lord Hanuman. "Love this big requires a sacrifice so important it may consume the river, as before with Agastya."

"He asked you?" said Kali.

"Yes," said Lord Hanuman.

"Me too."

"There must be sacrifice."

"There will be sacrifice."

"Yet I wonder. What if their love is too strong?"

"Then I will bite off the male's balls," said Kali, smiling, shaking the limp cat in her hand.

22 Asha Has Second Thoughts

Sitting in lotus position, next to an ancient Aghori sadhu, before a fire on the banks of the Ganges, Asha holds out the skull full of bhang.

"I don't like what Tishwali is becoming," Asha said.

The wrinkled hands of the man on his right took the skull and slowly brought it to his pursed lips. The old man's eyes, in the firelight, displayed forests of dead tree limbs encircling black holes. Solemn eyes of dark wisdom, of forbidden places explored, and repulsive deeds done without aversion.

"All that he has, and yet he craves more," said Asha. He took back the proffered skull and drank a large gulp of the intoxicating, hallucinogenic mix. He wanted to go far away from this reality. Away from the greedy schemes of his best friend.

"Yet he pledged new temples, yes?" said the old man.

"But more bank than temple!"

The old man scratched his foot. Spit into the fire. "His plan is proper. Aghoric. To turn the thing inside out. To show the hollow of what all think is solid."

"But his perversity is not based on our holy edicts. I fear he is simply becoming corrupt." Asha felt the fog rising inside him. He would lose himself soon, in the comforting fog.

"Bring him here. I will talk with him," said the old man. The fire popped. The both of them watched a flying ember zag about like a lovesick lightning bug.

"He won't come," said Asha, wiping an ashy tear from his cheek. "I can't reach him anymore." He studied his right palm, watched as the petals of his fingers slowly curled together, lost all track of time.

Asha's hand closed on little Tishwali's as the young boys snuck from their hard flat beds in the incense-filled ward, past the sleeping guard. Asha lifted the latch to open the big wooden door, Tishwali was too small to reach it. Asha held the door in both hands as he coached it open, trying to keep its hinges from squeaking. Leaving the door ajar, they walked down the steps of the ghat and left their monk boarding school for the last time. They would be on their own from now on. That is what both of them wished.

Walking far enough to not fear the hand of the head monk

on their necks, they finally sat at the river's edge. The whole city slept.

"I'm hungry," said Tishwali.

"We'll get by," said Asha. "Even the dogs survive by themselves." He pointed down the river where a pack of dogs snuck bones from the crematorium.

"I won't eat dead people," said Tishwali. "Only Aghoris do that."

"No they don't," said Asha. He did not think so anyway, despite their love of ashes and skulls of the dead.

A light rain began to fall, first refreshing, then cold on Asha's bare arms.

They ran up the steps, into the deserted city streets. "There!" said Asha, pointing to an abandoned temple where a dog had just slipped through a hole in the shattered door.

They climbed through the hole themselves, on their hands and knees. Took a moment for his eyes to adjust. Lights shining in the near corner slowly took the form of the heads of dogs. Asha noticed, fearfully, a low growling. He put little Tishwali behind him. Only to discover the gleam of faces in the opposite corner. Men in robes, sitting on the floor, absolutely still. Wasn't growling he'd heard at first, but a deep chanting from these holy men. Sadhus. Aghoris probably! Taboo breakers. Cannibals?

"Are they going to eat us?" asked little Tishwali, wrapping his arms around Asha's stomach.

"I don't know," said Asha.

But no, they were not eaten. The Aghori sadhus broke off their chant, and invited the boys over, offering them boiled potatoes and a mat to lay on. For several months Asha and Tishwali tagged along with the Aghori sadhus, taking lessons from them, learning how the world is all illusion and what is true today is false tomorrow. That there is no there, there. Nor here, here. Nor blink of a moment. Nor endless time.

Asha thought these were the wisest men on earth, and vowed to follow them, to learn what he could of their wisdom. Tishwali grew bored and got a night job at the crematorium as an untouchable, flushing the ashes and left over bones of the dead into the Ganges, after picking out any jewelry or gold teeth for the crematorium boss. Asha hired on as well.

Years passed. Asha became an Aghori adept, while Tishwali simply got adept at hiding the hot jewelry and gold teeth of the dead in his own mouth, hoarding in this way a small fortune that eventually they used, with the help of the adult Aghoris, to buy the rundown temple and establish a small bank for the poor.

Those were the best of times. And during those middle years he was the most proud of little Tishwali, a self-made businessman, barely twenty. No one gave more food to the parade of little monks than banker Tishwali. No one bothered to loan rupees to the poor like banker Tishwali, rupees for weddings, rupees for funerals, rupees for a used tuktuk with which to make a living.

Asha loved Tishwali and admired his stealthly business sense. They had grown up together, shared what little food they managed to beg, in the beginning, at the monk school where both their parents had abandoned them. They had spent so many long nights at the crematorium as children then teenagers doing the work of the lowest of the low, brushing the burned dead into the Ganges, while sharing their thoughts and their dreams. And they had spent years together struggling to make their small temple bank a success. Tishwali married, fattened up, while Asha was happy to live the solitary life of a holy man when not helping Tishwali at the bank.

Together they had created much from nothing, proving one of the most important Aghori edicts, that much really is nothing and nothing can be much.

Asha loved Tishwali as a brother and he would never betray him or let him down. Yes he would help Tishwali with his latest plan, even if it did possibly involve the taking of a life. A sacrifice, if you will, for the greater good. But his heart was not in it. He realized this as his body began to float, then drift down, as light as a feather. The warm earth kissed his cheek, and he fell asleep by the fire, a fire slowly dying. He dreamed, darkly, that he was a shadow, lost, searching for his body.

23 Are You OK?

"Fernanda? Can you say that again? The connection is so bad."

"*Yo dije*, how are you doing all alone? *Tan solo.*"

"Awful," he told her. "I wish you were here."

"I'll be there in a few days. I really think this place is good for me. I will be a better woman for you, you'll see, when I get back."

Silence.

"Randy?"

"Sorry, I was just thinking."

"Thinking what dear?"

"Nothing. I miss you, that's all." They talked for a few more minutes, about what they would do when they got back to the states. Was it time to have a baby? "Perhaps," he told her.

"I love you," she told him.

"I love you too."

Fernanda hangs up the phone, leaves the office and goes to her room for her hat and sunglasses. She leaves the ashram, goes and sits, lotus position, outside on the meditation platform overlooking the river. A cool mountain breeze softens the bite of the sun. She hums "Ommmmm" while trying to clear her mind, but memories come to her, memories of when Randy first stole her across the border.

The plan had gone beautifully up to that point, all those years ago. Randy had driven, with Fernanda curled in the trunk, a good 30 miles past the border crossing, out where the road runs through nothing but scrub and cactus. He parked on the side of the road, put on the blinker lights, and quickly freed Fernanda from the trunk when there were no headlights in sight. She kissed him and hugged him. They both laughed with relief.

Then they waited, sitting in the open mouth of the trunk, enjoying the desert night. They watched a train pass, counted its cars, 232.

An old rancher in a white Ford pickup slowed to a stop beside them. The man lifted his cowboy hat in greeting, asked through his open passenger window if he could help.

"Just letting her cool down," said Randy.

"She does look pretty hot," the rancher said, nodding to Fernanda and winking to the both of them. His tires slid as he pulled away, dinging their feet with gravel.

"Chance is a risk taker," said Randy.

"How does he know so much about marijuana?"

"He used to drive up to Arkansas, to get pot for his sick mom. From a place called Noah's Ark. People don't know but pot helps sick people. Course he always got extra. To use and to sell. Chance ain't no drug dealer though. He's really a good person. I hope he makes it across."

"He will come," she said. And she was right. In less than an hour, Chance pulled up, looking no worse for his tangle with customs and immigration.

"They found a couple seeds between the seats," explained Chance. "Not enough to charge me."

"You got lucky," said Randy. "What if they'd found an old lid you'd misplaced? You'd be sitting in jail for years." He gave a big sigh of relief. "Let's drop Fernanda in town up ahead, then turn around and take the Gran Fury back to Fernanda's uncle."

He started to close the trunk.

"Not so fast," said Chance, stopping the motion. "I got

something to get from the spare well."

He twisted off the nut, lifted the metal cover, and voila, in place of the Gran Fury's spare tire were six tightly wound packages of Mexican pot. He grabbed the pot and threw it in the trunk of his old Chevy.

"What the hell!" said Randy. "Where did all that come from?"

Chance hung his head. "I told you I made a good contact in that Mexican jail. You'd be amazed how cheap I got it."

"Oh hell, Chance! I can't believe you let me drive through customs with enough pot in the car to get me twenty years! Twenty frigging years in federal prison!" Randy circled Chance, yelling in his face. "Wasn't enough that I was smuggling a person, you had to make me smuggle drugs as well? Why didn't you just buy a gun and shoot me!" Randy slammed the Fury's trunk.

"I helped you with your damn wetback, didn't I?" countered Chance.

"Get the hell out of here!" said Randy. "I can't trust you. I could never trust you."

"Alright," said Chance. "If you want to play that way. I'm gone. Dallas. Arkansas. Look out world!" He got in his car and slammed the door.

"Fernanda, get in your uncle's car," said Randy. "We'll return to Laredo, park it near the bridge. We'll take the greyhound to Dallas."

Fernanda did not move.

"You have no money," she said, finally. Her eyes looked north. "Immigration checks the bus."

"We'll figure that out," he told her.

"Let's take the car to Dallas," she said. "Let's take the Fury."

"We can't steal your uncle's car. Not after he was so nice to let us borrow it. Anyway, the plates are hot. Come on." He tried to take her arm, but she dodged his grip.

Chance started the motor of his mom's Chevy, turned on the headlights. He hesitated, pulled onto the roadway slowly, practically crawling, waiting for them to stop him.

"I'm sorry," Fernanda said as she broke into a mad dash, in the middle of the road, behind Chance's tail lights, waving and yelling for him to stop. Chance slammed on his brakes. She jumped in.

"*Vamanos*," she said.

"But," Chance said, looking at a tiny Randy in his rearview. She punched him in the shoulder and repeated "*Vamanos!*"

Only a hundred miles later, as the thousand lights of San Antonio broke the horizon like a city appearing from the future, from her brand new future, did Fernanda shed a tear for Randy.

In Rishikesh, sitting in the sun, before the holy Ganges, Fernanda remembers her betrayal, and even though they eventually got back together, her and Randy, she can never forgive herself for what she did to him that night. Maybe she does deserve to be sacrificed, after all. Maybe that will be her just reward for betraying Randy.

24 Randy's Dilemma

"So you spoke with her and everything is fine?" asked Julie.

Above them an escaped kite flew cross the river, like a spirit, flittering, flittering. A wonderful night to be on the roof of the hotel, in command of the river.

"I spoke with her and everything is fine with Fernanda," he said. "I'm sure she's enjoying mineral baths and stone massages. Everything is fine with her but not with me."

Julie put down her fork. "What's wrong with you? A problem at the bank this morning?"

"You know what I mean," he said. "Last night. We had sex."

"And so?" said Julie. "You seemed to enjoy it, last night, *n'est-ce pas?*"

He bit his lower lip. Yes, the forbidden memories of the night before had come back to him, while teaching at the bank in the morning, every kiss and caress and the wonder of it all. As much as he wished to blame the smoke, and blame God for bringing them together, still he knew he had to take full responsibility for their lovemaking. For making love with this incredible woman. A woman he had assumed was forever out of his reach.

A woman who should have still been off-limits, given he was now happily married with Fernanda. How could he have done what he had done? What kind of a man was he? He knew what he had done was a sin, and yet, at the time, it had seemed a holy act. Between two people in love. He knew he could not go on like this. That he would have to decide between them. But how could he? How could he choose?

I must never do it again, he told himself. I must never do it again. And I surely must never tell her that I want to do it again.

"I do remember," he told Julie, putting his head down. "And I loved every minute. And I want to do it again."

"Come," she said, taking his hand. "Let me make you late for work."

Afterwards, when he'd left, Julie went down to the ghat and sat on a step with a view of a bend in the river. Still high on the afterglow of love making, she let her thoughts wander. Back to Paris, back to the time Randy and she visited the Natural Museum at the Jardin des Plantes. They climbed a wide wooden stairway from the 1700s, of polished hard wood that had taken hundreds of years to grow in deep forest full of grunting boar and silent peering deer. She remembered feeling in her hand a rumble in the rail of the stairway, like deep breathing, as they climbed, as if the stairway were alive, allowing them sanctuary on its back. Allowing them a magic moment alone. She reached out and took Randy's hand. His hand enveloped her's with a safe, warm feeling. Suddenly she was swept away to another place, another time. She was the branch of a tree reaching out and touching another, after striving, in the wind, for hundreds of years. Dew fell on her hand. No it was a tear. She was crying with the joy of finally touching someone who could make her feel this way.

25 Reining In The Horses

"Pull in those free-running thoughts," Win tells Fernanda, who is not only fighting to stay balanced in her lotus position in the yoga hall of Harmony House, but also fighting off the news from husband Randy that Julie is still in Varanasi, that she never went to Khajuraho!

I believe she has the meeting on Monday, Randy told her on the phone, sounding unsure himself.

"Is something wrong?" she'd asked him, before saying goodbye.

"You left me."

"Oh you big baby!"

"I love you."

"I love you too."

Win thumped her forehead. "Turn off the thoughts!"

She let them go then, let go the thoughts, the cares, the worries, the weight of the past and the fear of the future. Counted the minutes then lost track of them as well. Did she fall asleep, sitting up? She is barefoot in a grand hall with a worn marble floor and granite columns, like a Catholic church she once visited in Mexico City, when she was a girl, traveling with her father and his Mariachi band. The stone is cool and smooth and she would like to lie down, feel her cheek press against the stone, to become stone herself.

A girl is standing by her in the dream, looking at her. She is a cute girl in a simple white dress.

"Are you the sacrifice?" the girl asks.

Fernanda does not know what to say.

"Follow me," the girl says, taking her hand. "I will prepare you."

"No," says Fernanda, suddenly frightened.

"There must be sacrifice. You or the other you," says the girl.

"*Que?* No, please," says Fernanda, trying in vain to free her hand.

"I said come with me!" the girl screams, her words shrieking in echo against all the stone that surrounds them, her hand squeezing Fernanda's with inhuman strength.

"No," says Fernanda, reaching with her free hand, caressing the girl's hair. "No, I'm not the sacrifice. Please let me go."

26 Another Invitation

"Yes," said Julie as she and Randy walked the ghats at sunset. This was her favorite time, after the departure of the pilgrims and hawkers, before the prayer shows, the Aarti ceremonies. A time of special moments: of kids flying their homemade paper kites impossibly high above the river, of swifts patrolling in unison the tower tops, of black water buffalo coming down the wide steps to take their evening bath in the river. "Yes, dear Randy, my meeting in Khajuraho is Monday. But I was thinking to fly down tomorrow. Spend the holiday weekend there." She stopped on the narrow step, reached out a hand to Randy's chest. "I was wondering if you would like to come with me? For the weekend."

Randy could sense emotion behind the request. Perhaps she feared he would say no. It was in fact his intention. Yet what was the alternative? There would be no more diving until Monday. And a weekend was too short to fly to Rishikesh, to be with Fernanda. No, his only other choice was to stay alone in Varanasi, walk the stinking crowded ghats alone each day, under the hot sun, all the time wishing that he had gone.

"I'd love to go to Khajuraho with you," he said. "But as a friend only. Separate rooms."

"Of course," said Julie, standing there, looking into his eyes, holding his shirt. "*Des amis.* Very good friends."

He stood before her, watching her face, loving the desire he saw there. He kissed her, hard on the lips, kissed her and it didn't matter who saw. He loved this woman. He had always loved her, from the moment he first saw her in Paris.

Randy was a firm believer in signs, and his stumbling upon her in Varanasi completely by accident was the clearest sign he'd ever seen. Obviously their love was meant to be. To deny it would dislodge the world, derail the natural order of things. He had to go with her!

They went to his hotel; it was closer than hers. They made love, on the unmade bed, she whispering in his ear, him catching only fragments – "Varanasi" – "city of light" – "meant to be" – "there, slower" – "faster" - "yes, please, yes!"

27 The Soul Of All Things

"The universe is alive," says Win, leading Fernanda on a hike through the Himalayan foothills, past farmsteads with stone pillared gates, past a man coaxing his buffalo to market, past a woman on the steep hillside with a basket on her back - the strap from the basket grips her forehead - a small scythe in hand, she chops vegetation and tosses the green strands over her shoulder into the basket, while thoughts form half-spoken words on her lips. Past children who voice their desires, they want candy – all children want candy; past tiered rice fields whose synchronized curves look musical; past a haystack sitting on a platform looking like a ghost. And often, in the distance, as they come to a high point, the immovable snow-covered summits to the Northeast strive for the heights of the weightless clouds in a thin blue sky.

"In the beginning of the end of another beginning," says Win, "of another end and beginning, ad infinitum, there was a point, dense with all things. This lone point, this God thing, made up as it was of all things, was lonely, and wondered if there was another of its kind in the infinite emptiness around it. So it divided itself, exploded across the vast emptiness, slewing out in all directions, looking for what we would call love."

"God was lonely?" asks Fernanda, winded. She sits on a small boulder next to the goat path. "Sorry, I have to rest."

Win sits next to her. He is handsome as ever but seems less serene today. She tells him so.

"Ha!" he says. "Women and their sixth sense. Yes, I am troubled today. By your dream. That is why I am telling you the story of the beginning."

"Oh," said Fernanda. "*Por favor*, continue."

"When all things split from God, in the beginning, there was much chaos. And this troubled God. He decided he would never succeed in finding Love if all inside was chaos, so he split his soul, what we would call a soul anyway, into controlling entities. He split his soul into forces that westerners know as physical laws but what early man and we Hindus, being an old people, still refer to as Gods. Gods like the pull of one body to another, like the cycles of procreation and death. A God of war and destruction, a Goddess of music and dance. A God of drunkenness, a Goddess of beauty. And Demons too. These Gods and Goddesses and Demons, the laws of nature as you westerners refer to them, are incarnations of God, the lone one in the beginning, the point that dared to expand and search for love."

The clouds coming over the summits billow. The air turns cool.

"Will he ever find his love?" asks Fernanda, rested now, rising to her feet.

"That isn't the question," says Win. "The question is will he ever grow tired of sacrificing his energy, his entire self – searching for love? Will he ever lose faith in the possibility of true love? Of love that lasts forever?"

They walk in silence for several minutes along a narrow path with a thousand foot dropoff to one side.

"So what has all this to do with me?" asks Fernanda. A single dark cloud spills cold drops on her head.

"I see but not clearly," says Win. "Interpreting your dream, getting to know your aura, I fear you are at the center of something of such importance, such significance, that the matters of all men and women in the world pale in comparison. It's almost as if you were at the center of the universe. Your own universe."

"That's what love does, doesn't it?" says Fernanda. "It creates its own universe around two lovers."

"I fear for that universe," says Win.

Fernanda feels the chill to her bones. What is he telling her?

How could he know? I'm losing my love? Is that it? Can it be? I'm losing Randy?

"What can I do?" she asks him. The sun tries to break through the cloud, but fails. At least the rain stops.

"What can any of us do? We are at the mercy of the Gods. And yet . . ."

"And yet what?"

"Sometimes, under the right conditions, one can defy the Gods."

What did he mean by this? she wondered. How did this comment apply to her own condition? Why did holy men insist on talking in riddles?

They make it back to the ashram just in time for Arti, the nightly ceremony of light. Julie lets her worries lift off like seabirds from the river. She jokes with Win, even tries to play a small copper horn along with the musical festivities.

"You are a natural," Win tells her, putting his arm around her waist. She can feel warmth of his body through the thin robe he wears.

"No," she says, taking the horn from her lips. "My father taught me. When I was a little rooster of a girl. My father raised me alone, you see. I never knew my mother. Father used to joke that I fell to him from the sky."

"You are a professional musician, then?" asks Win in surprise.

She likes that she can surprise this man who seems to know everything about her.

"I traveled all over Mexico, with my father's band. He even lost me one day in the ruins of Chichen Itza. When I was 7."

Win's face darkens. "Dear Fernanda, whatever happened to you there?"

"I don't remember clearly. That was so long ago. But I think 3 old Indians helped me. Gave me gifts. A handful of strong smelling herbs and a gold coin. An old Mexican *peso*, but in gold. I remember how upset my father was when he found me. He threw the herbs away and wept, and kept repeating something. I can't remember really. Except, except I do remember how pleased and puzzled he was when I showed him the gold *peso*. He said he would keep it for me. I suspect though he spent it right away."

Win laughs, then his expression turns serious.

"Tell me about these men, these Indians that gave you presents," he asks.

"Like I said, I don't remember much. They were nice. Maybe they worked there?"

"You know, Fernanda, that they practiced human sacrifice there, at Chichen Itza," says Win. "The ancient Mayans. Maybe it had something to do with that."

The music of the arti came to a crescendo, sputtered to chaos.

"Well I certainly wasn't sacrificed, if that's what you are implying," says Fernanda. "After all, I'm still here."

Win let go of Fernanda's waist.

"Sometimes they did not sacrifice the body," he says, turning his head away when she looks at him. The side of his face reflects the twinkling lights of the river as the music dies down. He turns back to her, sadness in those dark eyes in that dark face. "Sometimes, Fernanda, instead of sacrificing the body of the prisoner, the Mayan priest would sacrifice his soul."

Fernanda did not know what to think about that. Was he implying she no longer had a soul? He was wrong. She had a soul. And his name was Randy.

28 The Splendor Of The Temples Of Khajuraho

The town of Khajuraho reminded Randy of one of those sleepy towns out in the hill country west of Austin, Texas. A two lane paved road sliced the quiet town in half, while a second partially paved road split the town the other way making a kind of cross, an X marks the spot, the spot of Randy and Julie, a couple yet not a couple, recently arrived, walking in the crisp morning under a clear sky towards the western temples, the Kamasutra temples, the thousand year old temples with the pornographic sculptures.

This being a holiday, vendors manned booths and carts along the way to the temples, with fried pie, candy, jewelry and flowers. Randy bought a sugary pink chunk of peanut brittle, from a large stack sprinkled with flies. "Too early for candy for me," said Julie.

On the main street few cars passed – when they did they kicked up dust as they sped by, dust that took its time resettling. The locals walked to where they needed to go, or rode bikes. Families rode motorcycles - 3 kids in front and a wife and mother-in-law clinging to the back.

Across the way Randy noted an algae-choked lake; his mind's eye tried to make it picturesque, but failed. Tuktuk and pedal cab drivers called out but the temples were right in front of them.

Julie had told Randy about the temples, so he wasn't too shocked to see the acrobatic sexual positions depicted on the walls of the main temple in the western complex, the explicit trysts in the midst of the stone carvings as old as Notre Dame's gargoyles.

"Now that is a bit much," said Randy, stopping before a particularly explicit carving.

"Not to me," said Julie. "You Americans are such prudes." She moved close to him, facing him, her lips inches from his. Then just as he leaned forward, she turned away, leaving him longing.

They continued round the building.

The sheer number of intricate carvings, of strong gods and amply curved goddesses carved as if they were swaying, of geometric patterns and receding concentric blocks all piled on top of one another struck Randy as something quite harmonious and beautiful. He was so glad he had come to see them. The occasional sex depicted on the temple walls was key to the experience, just as the gargoyles and demons are key to the experience of Paris' Notre Dame. Because they don't belong there! And yet, somehow they do.

Aren't we all as incongruent, and mysterious, as the cathedral of Notre Dame or the temples of Khajuraho, with holiness and sexual cravings living side by side within us?

This is what Randy was trying to get his head around. Why was he so taken with Julie, when he already had a wonderful wife in Fernanda? Could he possibly have the two of them. Didn't Mexican men do this all the time, and French men as well? A wife and a mistress. But no, that was not his way. Of course he must choose one. No matter how much this hurt.

Randy and Julie took off their shoes and left them at the foot of the main temple. They climbed the steps in their socks and took in the view from the temple porch, to the smaller temples scattered about the complex. Such a quiet place. Holy place. They entered the cave cool interior and found more carvings, but with a denser, darker stone. Randy took Julie's hand.

"I can't see you after this weekend," he told her. There was much more he wanted to say, but he held back, afraid he would only make it worse. How could he tell her that he hated himself for betraying Fernanda?

Julie said nothing, reached to the stone arm of a statue that had been brushed by hands for a thousand years. A thousand thousand hands? Most gone now, turned to dust, but each touch had polished the stone arm a bit, a tiny bit, until, after a millennium, the arm gleamed in the dim light with an other-worldliness.

"A weekend can last forever," she told him. She leaned up and kissed his lips, lips that she tried to devour.

He kissed her back, hard, reflecting every bit of her hunger, of her desire. He couldn't explain this incurable hunger he suddenly felt for Julie, almost as if he were being manipulated by forces beyond his control. They were possessed, the two of them, and who knew how this would play out.

29 Secret Desire

The door to the tiny apartment in the colonial style building in the back alley behind Meer Ghat opened slowly. Neelu's face with that squarish jaw appeared. Her little head turned quickly side to side, like a chipmunk at the entrance to her hole. Her eyes sparkled. She sighed.

"It's ok," she said.

Mr Tishwali's corpulent figure filled the doorway, his elephant trunk of a beard swaying back and forth. His open-eyed look dared the world to judge him. He, who owned a bank. He, who dared install that bank inside a temple. He, who dared to do the impossible! Content and tired, he leaned down to kiss his lover on the cheek. He noticed, as he did so, the after-love glow in her eyes. He must appear to her, in his spotless white suit, a man of such wealth and new beginnings, he must appear like a veritable incarnation of Ganesh! As so he felt.

Yet they had argued, a bit, earlier, when he explained what they must do to ensure Randy's cooperation.

"But he volunteered!" she had protested. "I know he will comply with your wishes without such pressure. He is a good man. I see it in his eyes."

"Insurance," was how Mr Tishwali explained the need to Neelu as they stood beside the bed, disrobing. "This plan is about nothing if not insurance." He had embraced her and she conceded to his will.

Now he set off, refreshed, on a slow walk into the night, under the stars, not home, no, first to his beloved bank. Spotting only lone dogs and bone-thin teenagers, homeless, hungry, he remembered his own youth. How far he had come! From a shaved-head boy in orange robe begging for handouts with Asha, from the two of them sifting in the ashes of the dead for the treasures of the dead, now he and Asha dared reach for the treasures of the living!

Arriving finally at the bank, he greeted the night guard out front, a dark, half asleep, unarmed figure in a curled position on the sidewalk. Tishwali touched the man, "Don't get up," he said. "It's just me." He opened the padlocked gate with one key and the heavy wood door with another. He quickly locked the door behind him. He smiled, leaned down there at the entrance to touch the floor before the shrine of God Ganesh, grunted with the effort. Touched his forehead and thanked Ganesh for all the good that had come his way and all the good that would come if only Ganesh would help. He walked to the back, then, to the vault. He opened the vault, a heavy steel door, entered the room full of shelves, shelves full of rupees. He liked the smell of money. The sight of money. The sight of money. He did a quick inventory. Maybe 50 million? How much was that in dollars? A million? Enough to tempt even an American, surely. Enough to tempt a God!

30 Night Hunt

Not far from the bank, in the zigzag alleys of the ancient brick buildings of Varanasi, a teenage girl appears lost. She takes one turn, then another. Into the light, and back into the shadows. Backtracks, then forward again, until she stumbles across three men drinking on the porch of an abandoned building. They perk up to see her, one begins to stand.

"There you are dear," the man says. "I've been waiting all my lives for you!"

The girl panics, and turning from them, scraping her knuckles on the rough brick wall, somehow, she trips and falls.

They are on her like dogs on a bone at the cremation ghat.

They hold her down and the first one takes his turn.

"She is strange meat, this one," says the first. He finishes with a final thrust and pulls up his pants.

The second's turn comes. He says nothing, just pounds into

her. He screams when he finishes, surprising the others.

"Are you OK?" they ask him.

"I think so," he says, and they laugh.

Is the girl conscious still? They don't care. The third takes his turn.

Finishing, he starts to cry.

"What is it?" the others ask.

"I don't know," he replies. "I suddenly feel so sad."

They all three began to cry, standing over the inert body of the girl. And crying they all got very sleepy. They lay down beside the half-naked, beaten and abused girl, as if that were the most natural thing in the world to do after raping her. They lay together, on the ground in the dark back alley, next to their victim, and fell fast asleep.

The girl stirs, rises on her elbows. She looks over her attackers, not acting surprised at all by this strange spell that has overcome them. She turns over onto her hands and knees, climbs atop the first one and struggles to pull down his pants and then his underwear. Then, after some initial inspection, one by one, she bites off his balls.

31 Randy's First Kiss

Julie and Randy sat in a park in Khajuraho, the afternoon before their return flight to Varanasi, watching, in the distance, a soccer game on a barren field between neighborhood boys.

"Why?" asked Julie. "Why do you need to kiss before you can make love?"

"I don't know," said Randy. "Maybe something to do with my first kiss."

"Tell me," said Julie.

"It's a long story," he said. "To tell it right."

"We have all night," she said.

"No, I can't tell it."

"*Sil te plais?*" She gave him her sad poodle eyes.

"I can't tell it," said Randy. "But maybe we can act it out."

"*J'aime bien*," said Julie. "I was born to act."

"All right then, you'll be April. I'll be fourteen year old me."

"April was her name. April the ticket taker. I can still see her swinging free the heavy bar at the gate, allowing entrance to the Drive-in with its twin white billboard screens off Highway 75 in Dallas. Stand up and open the gate," he told Julie. Julie stood and pretended to open the iron gate. "You brush flakes of rust from your hands, crunching the gravel with your fake army boots."

Julie laughed and brushed imaginary flakes from her hands.

"Don't laugh. April didn't laugh."

"I'm sorry," said Julie. "I'll do better."

"Remember you are April the ticket taker, with her wise pained eyes and a long pony tail."

Julie raised her eyebrows and tossed her imaginary pony tail.

"A dollar a head, ticket taker April says, leaning out the ticket stall window towards the first car. Kids fifty cents."

Julie held out her hand. "A dollar a head. Kids fifty cents." Her French Texas accent grated on Randy's ear, but he let her play the part anyway.

"My brother Steve's car pulls up. I am hidden in the trunk of the mustang convertible. The eight track tape is blaring, the car jumps the curb. The metal clamps of jumper cables pinch my side and I yelp."

"Quiet! my brother calls from the driver's seat. You want her to hear you?"

"Steve's girlfriend back then, Karen, says, Don't worry we'll tell the money girl we have a rat in the upholstery!"

"You're the only Jesus-freaking rat I know!" Randy yelled, startling Julie. "We pull to the ticket booth, and you, April the ticket taker, peer down on Steve and his date."

"2 American dollars," Julie said, getting back into character. She held out her palm.

"We don't have any one in the trunk, Karen confesses to you," said Randy. "And you say, I didn't even suspect."

"I didn't even suspect, you all," said Julie.

"Good," said Randy. "Now tell us to get out of the car."

"I think I would like you all to open up the trunk," said Julie.

"Excellent. Your pony tail whips through the air as you drop from the stool, exit the booth and walk to the back of the car."

Julie walked to the back of the invisible car. In the distance the soccer game was breaking up, kids getting on their bikes and heading home before sunset.

"My heart beats louder in my ears with each approaching step. I'd never tried to sneak in before, so I didn't know what it was like to get caught.

The driver's door opens. Brother Steve gets out. His feet crunch in the gravel, with a tennis shoe sound, crunch crunch yet different from the crunch made by the heavy boots of April. The trunk pops open and out I spring, face spattered with oil, jumper cables caught on my waist and looping round me like the cord on a newborn baby. Startled at first, ticket taker April stares me down and shakes her head."

Randy jumped up, and Julie fell back a step.

"I squint at you, blink, my eyes adjusting to the light. Wild strands from your pulled-back hair halo in the rays of the setting sun."

"How old are you? you ask me," said Randy.

"How old are you, boy?"

"Fourteen, I say."

"A dollar," said Julie, in control now, moving back into her routine as gate keeper.

"Whatever thought my sudden oily appearance had stirred in you was now banished by your need to do your job."

"One U.S. dollar," Julie repeated in her role as April.

"I raise my hands, letting you arrest me if you want. If I'd had a dollar, I tell you, I wouldn't have been in the trunk."

"Sorry bro, says Steve as he hands ticket taker April 2 dollar bills, money for him and for Karen but nothing for me. He gets back in the driver's seat, as if I didn't matter. Guess you'll have to foot it home, he tells me. Then he drives the convertible into the theater parking for screen one, where the image is just now flickering, not quite distinguishable, like the subconscious shuffling its cards before dealing the night's dreams."

"That's a beautiful line," said Julie.

"I read it somewhere. About dreams."

"A dollar," repeats Julie.

"I watch, a young skinny lad," said Randy. "Abandoned to the fall of darkness, I watch as Steve and Karen drive over the grass humps of each row, passing carefully through the speaker posts with their twin speaker boxes, parking on the far side along the fence where the gang has started gathering." Randy pointed to the far goal in the open field.

"Ticket taker April eventually ignores me too, going back to her stool in the ticket booth."

Julie went back and sat on the bench.

"The line of cars snakes by you, while dollar bills and quarters pile up in the cash drawer."

Julie piled up imaginary money.

"The sky darkens and previews of 'Planet of the Apes' materializes on the twin screens. Ticket taker April jumps when she realizes I am sitting on a stump next to the open doorway of the booth, realizes that I never left her side."

"How long you been there? she says. I can still hear the twang in her voice."

"How long you been there, boy?" said Julie.

"Forever, I tell you. I remember examining the lay of your face and the intense liveliness of her eyes. 'Can I have a piece of your gum?' I ask you."

"No," Julie said. "You go away now. I have to work."

"Fewer and fewer cars enter," said Randy. "Ticket taker April has nothing to do but makes it a point not to look my way. By not looking at me, only a couple of feet from her legs, she hopes I will leave. But I am not going anywhere. Something about her has snagged me. I can't get free.

The opening soundtracks from both movies distort hundreds of box speakers hanging in car windows or propped on the back of pickup trucks parked in reverse, where their owners sit in lawn chairs drinking beer. The last light of the day drains behind the flickering screens, just like now, bringing into sharp contrast, into life, giant human forms playing out their stories against a black void."

"Isn't it wonderful, Julie?" said Randy. "Isn't it a wonderful night?"

"You mean, now?" said Julie, "or then?"

"Both."

"Watching movies is like watching tales of the gods, I blurt out to ticket taker April. You need to go away, she tells me in return."

"You need to go away," Julie said, but she passed me a piece of gum.

Randy smiled at Julie's improvisation.

"I smell her Juicy Fruit breath as she leans down. I take the stick of gum, strip off the foil and put the flat sugar-dusted piece into my mouth. I roll it up on my tongue and am pleased to share the taste in my mouth of what she herself is tonguing. We chew in silence, eyes going from one screen to the other, the words of the acting gods garbled so, we had to read their lips."

"You need a loud speaker in this booth, I tell you. You reply you don't usually watch anyway."

"Oh I don't usually watch anyway," Julie said.

"She opens the cash drawer and takes out a paperback, The Best Science Fiction Short Stories of 1969. Go away now and let me read, you tell me."

"Go away and let me read," said Julie, turning the page.

"I settle on watching screen one, a movie called Billy Jack, about some hippie commune next to a redneck town, where the rednecks beat up the hippies because the hippies want peace and the rednecks like war, or at least they don't want whatever the long haired hippies want. Then a War Vet, Billy Jack, trained in karate by the military, takes the side of the hippies, to everyone's amazement."

"Do you believe in The War? I ask ticket taker April."

"I don't know, replies April. My boyfriend does. He didn't even wait to get drafted. He signed up. Her face flinches. I feel a pinch in my gut, in sympathy with her."

"I don't know," said Julie. "My boyfriend likes the war so much he signed up." Her face flinched.

"I just don't see the point of The War, I tell you. But I wouldn't mind traveling there. I want to see the world. You, April, tell me there ain't any difference from here."

"Ain't no different from here," said Julie. "People are people."

"Are you going off to college?"

Julie thought a second. "I, I want to."

"Yes, she wants to. That is, you want to," said Randy. "That's why you are working here, to save up. But now something's happened, says April."

"What? I ask April. What's happened?"

"Nothing for you to know, she tells me, going back to her reading."

'Nothing for you to know," said Julie.

"Then the strangest thing happens. In the blink of an eye, with the switch of a reel, Billy Jack becomes The Abominable Dr. Phibes on the screen. And instead of kicking ass on rednecks he is laughing insanely as he murders doctors with plagues from the Bible. Right like that, right in the middle of the film. I look to screen two, and Billy Jack, the movie I thought I was watching, has jumped over to that screen. Car horns begin to honk. You step out of the booth and look around, saying, What's going on?"

Julie stands and walks a small circle, saying, "What's going on?"

"The movies jumped screens," Randy said. "Tell me you are going to inform old man Gus what happened."

"I've got to tell old man Gus what happened," said Julie, heading to the imaginary refreshment stand.

"Abandoned, I make my way inside the parking for screen one. I spot silhouettes of the gang as I walk down a gravel alley between two lines of cars, past smells of popcorn, beer and sweet smoke. The speaker boxes suddenly all crackle, interrupting the soundtrack, and a scratchy voice begins to speak. Its old man Gus, telling everyone to please switch parking areas to continue with their chosen film.

Loud cursing follows, a few horns honk, then most of the vehicles pack up and move to the alternate screen. But the gang from the high school doesn't bother to move. They aren't here for any particular film. They are here to hang out.

I recognize the parked car of my friend Chance. Well, Chance's mother's car. Chance was only fifteen but since his mother was dying of brain cancer he was allowed to use her car. Chance was a little crazy then, because of what was going on with his mother, but I enjoyed his antics."

"Hey Chance, no date tonight? I say, opening the passenger side to Chance's car to plop down."

"Nah, he tells me, but I got some great Colombian. You want to try it? Your brother Steve bought some."

"Colombian?" asked Julie. "You mean marijuana? At fourteen?"

"April?" said Randy. "You are April aren't you?"

"Yes, sorry."

"When I heard that Steve, my brother, when I heard that he had money after all, and could have paid my way to the movie, I felt betrayed as well as abandoned. I bark at Chance, No, I don't want any of your supposed Colombian. What I want is to kiss that ticket taker girl at the gate."

"I'd like to kiss a lot of girls, says Chance, lighting up. I've got beer in the back if you want."

"But I wasn't interested in beer either. I was interested in ticket taker April. I was interested in YOU. I wondered what it would take to win a kiss from such a girl."

"So you fell for the ticket taker?" said Julie.

"Shh," said Randy.

"I'm sitting there, in my friend's car, listening to the Best of the Fifties, thinking of April, thinking of you, while Dr Phibes pours honey on a beautiful woman's face and releases locusts to eat the honey and her face. Just then Chance breaks out singing to the song on the eight track, Oh where or where can my baby be, the Lord took her away from me. She's gone to heaven so I got to be good, so I can see my baby when I le-e-e-ave-a this-a world!"

"I love that song, Chance says. I hope one day I crash and kill my girlfriend so I can sing it as it should be sung, with the proper feeling."

"What a horrible thing to say, I tell him."

"Ok, maybe not die, just break her leg. So I can sing it right."

"Sing what? Where or where can my baby be, the lord broke her leg for me? I ignore Chance, sit and muse about ticket taker April so far away at her gate."

Julie slides to the far side of the bench.

"I'm going for a stroll, I say finally to Chance, opening the door."

"Chance grabs me by the shirt. No man, don't go. I need you to explain this fricking movie to me. First there's these hippies and then this War Vet beating up rednecks and then this deranged man in a tuxedo with no face killing people with grasshoppers. Like man, I am so lost!"

"The world is becoming like you, Chance, I tell him, and start to walk away, when I notice both tires on that side of the car. I walk to the other side and confirm that all the tires are flat. You know you got four flats, Chance?"

"Yeah, Chance says. Spent all my money on the Colombian. I had to sneak in the exit to the drive-in."

"Over those spikes? I say in disbelief."

"Yeah, Chance says."

"I shake my head. Every day Chance proves he is crazier than the day before. And there was nothing for it. Except for maybe his mom to die once and for all and his father to run away then Chance could get over his craziness. Maybe. As I walk away in the dark, I hear Karen's annoying nasal pronouncing Jesus is in every one of us. I begin to hum to myself, Oh where or where can my Jesus be, the Lord took him away from me."

"You appear in the distance, in your booth, and all is right with the night. I stride towards you, as the films on both screens end. The intermission cartoon comes on as I crunch my way towards the entrance."

Randy pretends to crunch towards the entrance of the drive-in movie theater.

"So when do you get to leave the booth? I ask ticket taker April."

"Why? you say, looking at me with interest, then catching herself and purposely turning away.

"Why?" said Julie, drawing her face close to Randy's, then looking away.

"I thought you might want to take a walk, that's all, I say. You reply that you have a boyfriend."

"I told you," said Julie. "I have a boyfriend. Anyway, you're too young."

Randy laughed.

"Who's out of character now?"

"Sorry," said Randy. "I told her I'm not asking her to go out. Though there is one thing I'd like, I dare to say. What? she says."

"What do you want from me?" said Julie.

"A kiss."

"April laughs, saying, That ain't going to happen. And by her tone I know she means it, but still I can't give up."

Julie said, "That ain't going to happen, boy."

"Intermission ends, and the second features start, a film about dinosaurs and cowboys, and another Vincent Price horror movie. Only a third of the cars remain for the second feature. I notice most of the cars with little kids have gone home. This is big kid time now. I am a big kid. On an impossible quest."

"You go and lock the entrance gate. I have to patrol, you say, getting the flashlight from the booth. It's during the second feature that the weird starts."

"You do not complain when I join you on patrol. I walk by your side but try to keep out of your way since I know you are still on duty.

When the second features jump screens again, when a cowboy on a horse roping a T-rex is replaced suddenly by a mad host laughing cruelly as one of his guests perishes horribly, only a single car honks. Once. There is no announcement. No one bothers to start their car and drive over to the other screen, to follow their movie. Didn't really matter. When they were out of it, as most everyone in the parking lot was by now, one story, however fractured, was as good as another."

"A commotion brings ticket taker April, brings you, and me, over to 'the group'. My friend Chance is stumbling around his car, arcing full beer cans in the direction of the screen."

Randy became Chance, hurling heavy beer cans towards the sky.

"Chance curses, but apparently has bit his tongue, because it sounds like 'Fluck this flucking flilm! I just can't flollow it!'"

"Your friend Chance was drunk," said Julie.

"Chance was, and is, simply crazy," Randy said.

"Where was I? Oh yeah. You, April, are lecturing a perplexed Chance that he has to leave or you will call the cops."

"I'll call the cops!" shouted Julie.

"I intervene, show you that Chance's car has four flat tires. I know him. He can't help it. His mom is dying, I tell you. As you take in my explanation, another commotion catches your eye. It is Steve's girl Karen. She is standing in the seat of the convertible, standing with her arms outstretched, yelling 'All us women are crucified! Crucified for the sins of our stupid boyfriends!'"

"A man in the back of a nearby pickup yells for her to shut up and sit down."

"She can't handle the Colombian, explains brother Steve, pulling at her waist, trying to get her to sit."

"Fluck that, says Chance. Give her a beer to flix her."

Randy, as Chance, flung an imaginary beer at Steve's imaginary Mustang. Throws his hands up and makes a pa-toosh sound as it hits the imaginary car.

"Brother Steve curses Chance, and pulls Karen down before you kick them out. Then you and I corral a wobbly, foul-smelling Chance to the ticket booth, where he curls onto the wood floor mumbling that the world makes no sense. No sense at all. That who is me and who is you? He makes it a drunken song. There in the dark. I can almost see him in the dark." Randy points to the dark barren field. Not a soul.

Randy sat silently.

"I've never met your brother," said Julie. "I'd like to."

"He's in the military, overseas," said Randy.

"So did you get your kiss?"

"Yes let me continue. The movies end on the screens, replaced by long reaching circles of headlights as the patrons drive off the grass humps, down the gravel alleys and out the exit. The humid black Texas night envelopes the three of us in the ticket booth. I peer out on the sparkle left behind in the gravel, the candy wrap and the flattened beer cans. I am reminded, for no reason, of popcorn shell stuck between my front teeth. And I can't get it out."

"Is his mother really dying? you ask in a hushed voice, your hand reaching down and brushing a curl from Chance's innocent face."

"Is his mother really dying?" said Julie, speaking softly. The candlelight in the windows of the homes in Khajuraho could be a thousand years old.

"Yes," said Randy. "His mother is dying."

"We have to take him home, you say."

"We have to drive him home."

"Yes."

"Help me, you say."

"Help me."

"Together we haul Chance to April's beat-up Pinto. With Chance sprawled on the backseat, we leave the drive-in and head to his house. We set Chance in his doorway, with the hope that he will wake and go inside before being discovered by his parents.

On the way to my house, as I guide, you turn and you tell me, 'I think I'm pregnant.' Just like that. Out of the blue.

Julie hesitates. "I think I'm pregnant."

Randy is hot. Wipes the perspiration from his forehead.

"So there we go, driving across town, ticket taker April and me, sitting with my hands in my lap, wondering why you've confessed to me that you are pregnant. I'm certainly not to blame. What do you expect of me, so young? That's a good thing, right? To be pregnant? I finally get the nerve to say to you."

"No, you tell me. You say your boyfriend doesn't love you this way. That's why he joined the army."

"No," said Julie. "You see, my boyfriend, he doesn't love me now that I'm this way. That's why he volunteered for The War. He just wanted to kiss me, and, you know. He never wanted a baby!"

"You start to cry."

"No," said Julie. "I won't cry." But she couldn't help it. She knew the story too well.

"I bite my lip. All I'd wanted was a kiss, just like her boyfriend. But now there is a baby! Your boyfriend is a rat, I tell her."

"You look at me suddenly, releasing a moment your foot from the gas. I'm thinking to have an abortion, you say. I glide along, your words sinking in. You wince and turn your head to the street before us. The car speeds up."

"I'm thinking to have an abortion," said Julie.

"So there I am, sitting in the car with pregnant, heartbroken April, with you, telling me things I did not want to hear. All I had wanted from you that night was a kiss!"

"Here, I say. The house where the light is on. This is my home."

"You pull in front, hitting the curb, jolting the two of us.

I sit there in the seat, transfixed, not able to leave you. Then, as calmly as I can, my voice trembling, I say, If you don't want the baby, give her to me. I'll take care of her."

"I see you convulse and I worry my words have had the

opposite effect."

"You told her you'd take her baby?!" said Julie, incredulous.

"Yes, I told her that. Yet even today I don't know that I meant it. Or could have done it." Randy took a deep breath, coughed, and continued.

"I am sitting there in ticket taker April's front seat, watching her, watching you, shake silently, waiting for your response to my offer. I watch as a tear rolls down your cheek, a tear you do not bother to wipe. You release the steering wheel, at last, and turn to me. To my surprise, you break into a smile."

Julie tried to smile.

"Your eyes glisten, your smile fades. You whisper, Come here. I move towards you, slowly, the hair on my arms standing up. You lean down, lean down and over in a way no one has ever approached me before, up really close. Your eyes are enormous, glistening."

Julie leans close to Randy.

"You kiss me on the lips, a kiss full of hello and I love you and goodbye. My first kiss."

Julie smashed her lips against Randy's. He tasted her hot tears. Hello, I love you, and goodbye, Julie expressed with her kiss.

He staggered from the bench, steadied himself, dizzy, excited, facing her. She appeared before him young, scared, pregnant.

"That's okay, April tells me. I'll manage, you tell me. You pull the passenger door shut, straighten up, and I watch helplessly as you drive away."

"I hate you," said Julie, rising to her feet. Then she threw her arms around him.

32 I've Changed My Mind

Julie lay in Randy's arms, in the bed, in the hotel in Khajuraho. They have just made love a second time. The fan felt good on her naked body. She noticed the air is full of the smell of their love making. Of body juices and sweat.

"I've changed my mind," said Randy.

"About what?" said Julie. "*Dis-moi.*"

"About us. *Nous deux.*"

"Oh?" She turned and played with the hairs on his chest.

"I've decided."

"What have you decided?"

"That it is you that I want," said Randy, his voice cracking. "I want you. I love you." She hugged him with all her might, pressed her face against his chest. Smelled him.

Randy continued, "I feel we belong together. What else could it mean, this miracle meeting after years apart? It wasn't chance that brought us together. God brought us together."

Julie burst into tears. This is what she had planned for. This is what she desired to hear more than anything else in the world. So why did it hurt so much? Why did she feel so terrible?

"What is it? What's the matter? Did I say something wrong?"

"No, of course not. It's just that . . . I'm so happy . . . that God brought us together." And she cried that much more.

33 Kali Is Jealous

All this love! And none for me! Kali kicked a sleeping dog on the steps of the ghat. The dog squealed, instinctively started to bite but noticed the passing figure had no smell. Unnatural. The dog whined and curled up tighter.

I could love better than any human, thought Kali. I'm sure of it. But how, how does one love? How can I learn?

All she knew was seduction, inevitably followed by the bloody act that had fallen out of favor these past thousand years. Once men begged to be castrated so they could live in luxury, guarding the emperor's harem. Other men gladly castrated themselves so they could be free of devilish desire, thinking God would more readily embrace them. But all that was fading now. Half of what she stood for had fallen out of favor. Somehow she needed to change. Stand for something new. Love was today's blessing. Instead of being the Goddess of Seduction and Castration, she decided, somehow she needed to change herself into the Goddess of

Seduction and Love.

She looked for another dog to kick but none lay close. So instead Kali spat into the starry heavens reflected in the Ganges.

34 A New Beginning

Fernanda is lying on her back at the combination ashram and health spa in Rishikesh, lying on the thin mattress in her room, lying in the dark, listening to the muffled rapids, to a call from someone down by the river.

She is breathing heavily, having just awakened from another dream of the girl, the girl who wants to sacrifice her. Luckily she remembered, even while dreaming, what Win taught her, to take control of the situation, to stop going along for the ride.

She slows her breathing, and practices sending blood to different parts of her body, to her hand, to her foot, she concentrates and in time feels the heat of the extra blood in each location. She dares to concentrate on her vagina, remembering the fakir across the river. She wonders if she could ever be so in control of her body, ever so in control of her emotions that she could bring herself to climax with mere thought?

35 How Do I Tell Her?

Back in Varanasi, early in the morning, Randy walked the long line of ghats, away from the smoking ghat of the dead, upriver, past orange cloaked holy men awakening from small temples and holes in the ghat walls, men stripping and entering the river, ritually bathing the soul, then pulling out soap and sudsing the body as well.

Watching the sadhus wash themselves in the holy water, Randy felt his resolve to tell Fernanda that he'd fallen in love with Julie washing away as well. How could he tell her such a thing? How could he knowingly break her heart? With a phone call no less.

Returning to the hotel, he called her. She was a long time coming to the phone.

"*Que pasa, mi amor?*" she told him.

"I, I just wanted to hear your voice," he said. He had it all in his head, this conversation, how he would tell her to fly home because he was going to stay in India, maybe forever. For he had found someone that he loved even more than her. But he could tell her none of that. It wasn't true anyway, he realized.

"I think we should have a baby," he told her instead.

"What?"

"A baby. You mentioned it the other day. And I've been thinking about us. And I think a baby would be good for us."

"What does that mean? Good for us? That's no reason to have a baby."

"I mean, a good thing. For us, for the world."

"*No entiendo*," she said. "Are you OK? Is something the matter?"

"I'm just sleepy."

"I've got to go now," she told him. "Morning breathing exercises."

"Ah yes, we must remember to breathe, else we forget."

"What? Sorry, they are calling for me."

"That's fine."

"Love you."

"Love you too."

36 Kali's Kids

"Why is it so hard for him to decide?" asked the all-devouring goat of Lord Hanuman, from their vantage point atop the ancient water tower.

"Perhaps he loves them equally," Lord Hanuman replied. "Or equally does not wish to hurt them."

"He is a fool," said the goat.

"As are all who fall in love." Lord Hanuman's eyes were better than any mortal man's, yet still, no matter where he looked, he could not locate Kali. "Where is she?" he asked his goat.

"Hiding from us," said the goat. "Obviously."

"I wish to speak with her."

"Perhaps she does not wish to hear from you. I think she's back to her old tricks, that one."

"I know, as I know she cannot help herself."

"Trouble," said the goat. "She will bring trouble on those we watch."

"I know," said Lord Hanuman, crossing his arms. "Kali births trouble and death wherever she goes."

37 Over His Head

Randy met Raj, the turtle biologist, near the smoldering fires of Manikarnika Ghat. A pack of dogs, largely tame like all the animals in Varanasi, still they barked and snapped at each other, drawn by the smell of cooking flesh. They made Randy uneasy.

"Ah Mr Volunteer," said Raj. "I am so glad to see you have decided to attend another dive with me. Here, help carry these air bottles."

"I wouldn't have missed it for the world," said Randy. Anything to get his mind off his love trouble. To escape from the frighteningly real world above, to the terrifying surreal world below.

Together they made three trips up and down the wide ghat steps, bringing air bottles to both the storage shed and the boat from Raj's small truck. Then they suited up and climbed into the boat, with Raj taking the oars. Randy liked the occasional clunking sound of the oars against the sides of the boat, the splash of the water as the oars turned over.

Again early morning fog shrouded the river and caressed the ghat as they made their way out, until the fires on the ghat appeared like shrouded demon eyes.

"For a holy city, this place sure can look spooky," said Randy.

"All in the mind," said Raj. "All is in the mind."

Raj helped Randy over the side, with a splash, then followed him in.

The water felt colder than last time. Randy shivered, knowing the river started hundreds of miles away as snowmelt.

Down they went, into the green murk. Randy adjusted the air in his BC, pressurized his nose, and cleared a bit of water from his mask. They followed the anchor line down, to the mountain of bodies underwater, to this graveland of the innocents.

Randy spotted his first turtle, looking as big as a car, gliding over a mound of skeletons whose flesh had been picked clean. He felt a chill, not from the cold water but from the incredible image. He felt blessed to be allowed to experience such a place. This trip to India had been so far a true blessing. He loved Fernanda and he loved Julie and he had no idea what to do next about it, but what a rush to be in the middle of such a remarkable adventure. To have 2 women that wanted him. When he was young he had worried he would never even find one.

Raj motioned towards a group of smaller turtles, none of

which appeared to be tagged. They set about their work, while the turtles largely ignored them, too busy peeling milky molding flesh from the corpses in this spot. Randy tried not to look at the human faces, tried not to imagine the lives and deaths of these people who had become bottom feed. But thoughts did come to him, rose to him from below, thoughts of love affairs and tragic outcomes, of unexpected disease that ravaged good lives, of murders even. He could not help himself, he let his mind feed on the dead as well.

The dive invigorated Randy; he was almost sad to leave the river and go to work at the bank. To return to the living.

"Ah there is the man of the hour," announced Mr Tishwali, his monster hand enveloping Randy's. "We have much to do today, much indeed. For I want you to stage a robbery of the bank."

Randy took a step back, tried to smile. "What do you mean?"

"Come to my office," said Mr Tishwali. Randy followed.

"Please close the door." Randy did so.

"My partner and I want to test how well this new banking system from IBM can audit irregularities. I believe I mentioned this to you before. We want to do a test, where you basically pretend to be an inside hacker and create a bogus account in your name – you can do this yes?"

Randy frowned. "Yes I can do that."

"Excellent," said Mr Tishwali. "Then we want you to code transfers of all of the depositors' money into your bogus account."

"All?" asked Randy. "Why not just one? One would be enough to show the audit trail pointing back to me."

"Do you think a crook would stop at transferring only one depositor's account?" asked Mr Tishwali. "Oh no I think we must go all the way with our test robbery, otherwise it isn't real at all!"

Randy bit his tongue. He almost told Mr Tishwali this was a stupid idea, but then his consulting genes kicked in. The customer pays the bill so the customer is always right.

"So," said Mr Tishwali, "can you do this today, before closing? I want to reconcile all the money back into everyone's account just after we print off the audit and confirm we have caught our bandit."

"I can do it," said Randy. "I am uneasy doing it, but I can do this if you wish."

"I do wish," said Mr Tishwali. "In fact I insist. We must prove the new banking system is solid."

Why do I feel I am no longer in control, thought Randy. If I am not in control though, who is?

38 It Wasn't The Gods, It Was Me

Randy had lunch with Julie, pizza of all dishes, at a tourist place on the main avenue in old town.

"What are we going to do?" asked Julie, picking at her food.

"We could run off. Travel the world together, you and I," said Randy, half serious. At the same time he knew he must cut her off. He must end, once and for all, their affair.

"I'd follow you anywhere," said Julie.

"You followed me here," said Randy.

She winces – he is too close to the truth. I must tell him, she thought, the sooner the better. I must tell him that I loved him so much, that I needed him so much, that I arranged for him to come to India so I could prove we were meant to be together. For we are meant to be together. Dammit we are!

But she told him nothing. She feared he would stop loving her, if he knew, that he would never kiss her again. She feared the end of them.

Julie reached over and kissed Randy savagely, released him reluctantly, let him return to the bank still unaware of her trickery. I will tell him, I will, she told herself as she wandered aimlessly through the streets, through the throngs of locals, his taste still on her tongue. She floated through the mass of people living their small lives, hiding their own secrets and treachery, longing for love or worried of losing what love they had.

She remembered the first time she realized that she couldn't live without him. A month after Randy had left Paris, left because he thought she was unobtainable, Julie sat at a long wooden table in a meeting room at her company in downtown Paris. The discussion centered on a new project, plans were being laid, critical deliverables argued, staffing decided, when suddenly Julie realized she would never again hear Randy say her name. She realized that she would never again see the joy in his eyes when he spotted her stepping from the metro. Never again sit with him in a dark theater, daring to take his hand. Never again walk Montmartre with him as the artists packed up and the sun went down in great splotches of pink and golden paint. She had screamed in the boardroom that day. She wanted to scream now in the street. For it was starting all over again. The terrible feeling of loss. The loss of the love of her life.

Sometime later she found herself standing next to a huge brahma bull, in the middle of the street. She couldn't stop herself from reaching out and petting the beast's neck. How was it possible that all the animals in Varanasi were tame, loving almost? Was it something in the air? Was there a naturally higher level of consciousness in Varanasi, even in the animals?

The bull moved, waking Julie from her reverie. She watched him lumber towards the river, stopping traffic as he went. A beast of great weight and dignity. She followed him as he made his way down the steps, watched him poop on the bottom step before he entered the river. She sat a few steps above him, and contemplated him. Why can't we humans live so carefree? She checked her watch. Randy would be off soon, the bank closed at 4. She made up her mind to tell him the truth, took out a piece of paper and a pen and began to phrase her confession. She struggled with how to express to him that it was not the Gods that had brought them together in Varanasi, but her undying love for him. The words that came to her weren't perfect, but she felt better after writing them.

Completing the note, she climbed the steps, and made her way to Randy's hotel. A strange hotel, all cock-eyed. She found the room, and slid her note to him under the door. God she hoped this wasn't the end. That he would understand and love her even more for doing what she had done, once he'd digested the feelings behind the note. All out of love, she'd done it, all out of love for Randy.

In the lobby she was surprised to see that peculiar-looking

young woman from the party. That Neelu girl, who worked at the bank.

"Oh I was just asking at the counter for you," she said, shaking Julie's hand. "Randy told me to bring you to my place. He is to meet us there as soon as he finishes work."

"OK," said Julie, thinking it a bit strange, but if that was what Randy wanted. At least she would see him one more time without him knowing the truth.

She walked side by side with Neelu, through the afternoon shoppers. They passed a construction site where a man was piling bricks atop his head. A toy seller offered her a tiny spinning Ferris wheel. A goat ate a bag strapped on the back of a bicycle. She enjoyed this quick mini-tour of a part of the city she had not seen. It wasn't until they entered the small apartment, and the thin holy man came out of nowhere with a fat pipe and blew, again and again, that strange black smoke into her face, and she coughed and backed away towards the door to escape but the door was locked and Neelu was holding her arms, keeping her in place, saying, "It's ok, you'll be fine, just relax," it wasn't until then that Julie realized she had walked into a trap.

39 Win Loses

Fernanda quickly grew fond of her teacher, Win. He helped her with her confidence. Helped her feel she could manage what needed controlling in her life. "Follow your heart," he'd told her, "Even if it means defying the Gods."

Maybe it isn't Randy who is drifting away from me, she thought. Maybe I am drifting away from Randy?

Afternoon break found her restless. Thinking of Win. She sits down in the floor of her room in lotus position and tries to concentrate on nothing, but she can hear Win's voice in her mind's ear, a voice that gives her strength to battle against any comer. To fight off any nightmare. She wonders if she is falling in love with Win.

She imagines what it would be like to make love with such a man, a man who could control his sex like no other. She feels the blood then, collecting round her own sex. Her body spoke to her, her body wanted the touch of a man. She gets up, opens her door, and walks the long stone hallway to Win's room.

She pauses at the door. Starts to knock, but notices the door is slightly open. She hears a strange sound then, a sound that excites her. A kind of love moan.

She opens the door, sees a shadow leap off of Win, who is on his back, in bed. She steps into the semi-dark room, feels a rush of wind pass her out the door. She approaches Win, who is struggling to open his eyes, moaning louder now, coming to his senses, lying there naked. He reaches towards his groin. Fernanda looks down at where he is reaching and as her eyes adjust she can just make out the tear in his ball sack and the blood collecting and his left testicle lying by itself, further down, next to his knee, looking like a peeled, discolored, hardboiled egg.

Someone, some thing, had half-castrated Win.

40 The Robbery That Wasn't That Was

"So are we ready for the simulated robbery?" asked Mr Tishwali, five minutes before closing. "I would like to start this now."

Randy, sitting at the console in the computer room, nodded and pressed enter to launch the program he had just finished coding. A program that first created an account in his name, and then launched a background job of transferring all the money from all the existing accounts into his bogus account. Of course this was all done electronically, the money in the safe did not go anywhere. This gave Randy some assurance.

After only a few seconds, Randy was able to show Mr Tishwali his balance on the screen, 95 million rupees, much more than what was in the safe but that was normal – a bank never had all its depositors' money on hand.

"Excellent," said Mr Tishwali. "Now show me the audit trail."

Randy pulled up the audit screen, showed how the computer had successfully made note that his user id had made the bogus account and transferred all the money into that account.

"And you cannot change the audit? Put someone else's name?" asked Mr Tishwali.

"Wouldn't make any difference if I did," said Randy. "The audit log is replicated automatically offsite. Now can we reverse the transactions?" asked Randy.

"No," said Mr Tishwali. "The robbery is not over. You must first withdraw the money." Mr Tishwali handed Randy a note and walked out the door of the computer room.

Stunned, Randy sat there wondering what Mr Tishwali meant. He opened the note. A simple note, it said, "We have your spouse. Withdraw all the money and bring it to us in the backpack provided to Manikarnica Ghat. Or something terrible might happen."

"They've got Fernanda? Is this a joke?"

He ran after Mr Tishwali, but there was no sign of him in the bank. He tried the manager's door but the office was locked. A clerk politely informed Randy that Mr Tishwali had left for the day.

Randy puzzled over the note. Should he take it seriously? To be on the safe side, he asked a clerk to dial for him the long distance number to the health spa in Rishikesh.

He said hello and asked for Fernanda. The excited voice on the line told him sorry, that there had been an incident. One of their teachers is in the hospital and Fernanda, Fernanda has disappeared. The person did not know anything else. Fernanda had just disappeared.

Randy's heart constricted. So this was no joke. No simulated robbery. They did have Fernanda. He would have to do a real robbery, for Mr Tishwali.

But what nonsense! He was no bankrobber.

How did he get into this mess? Sure, Mr Tishwali was eccentric, a professed thief since childhood, but could he also be a kidnapper? Could he be a murderer? Mr Tishwali's betrayal shocked and hurt him. That first phone conversation came back to him, where Mr Tishwali had practically insisted Randy bring his wife to India. Now he understood why!

What a complete screwup this whole project had become. He looked over the note again, returned to the computer room for the backpack it mentioned. He found an enormous one under the table. A black one. Now how was he supposed to get the money from the safe into that pack? Oh, yes, of course. He was supposed to withdraw it. For his bank account showed that he was very rich man. With money deposited from all the other accounts.

I am no bank robber, he told himself. I can't do this.

He took the backpack with him into the lobby, and, hands shaking, voice cracking, he called over one of the departing clerks.

"I have to make an urgent withdrawal," he told the man. "I have to empty my account." Randy passed the clerk his passport, his IBM badge, and a piece of paper with the account number.

"Sir, we've locked the doors. We're closed," said the clerk, a middle-aged man in a gray suit.

"Mr Tishwali wants me to make a large withdrawal," he said. "He doesn't care if the bank is closed. It is, after all, his bank."

"Oh yes of course, Mr IBM," the clerk meekly responded. He went behind the counter and logged back into the new system. The clerk froze though when he saw on the screen the amount of money in Randy's account. "This is so much," said the clerk. "Normally I could not do such a transaction." The clerk looked at Randy, hoping he would retract his request. Randy said nothing. The clerk continued, "Mr Tishwali did mention to us you might want to test the new system. Making withdrawals and such. Oh I wish Mr Tishwali were here." He went quickly over to another clerk who told him Mr Tishwali had left for the evening. He went then to the floor supervisor, who had the combination to the safe. He explained in Hindi the remarkable request Randy had made.

The supervisor came over.

"You know, sir, we do not even have that much money

onsite?" he told Randy.

Randy nodded, tried to calm down, to play the game. For Fernanda's sake. "Just bring me all you have. This is a test of the new banking system," he told them, trying to sound assuring.

The supervisor looked at the clerk, the clerk at the supervisor. They exchanged a few words in Hindi, obviously hesitant to give all the money in the bank to this stranger from IBM. "We have been told to cooperate with you, but still. . ." said the supervisor.

"If you like this job I suggest you do as Mr Tishwali has instructed. That you follow a simple legal request. Bring me my money!" He hollered. Would have strangled the two of them if they had hesitated another minute. But they didn't. They set off to the backroom. "Only large bills!" he called after them.

They returned with a pushcart full of rupees. Randy filled his backpack. They brought another pushcart full. The few clerks left stood staring with big eyes. Randy stuffed in all he could, had to leave a thousand bills on the counter.

"Your tip," he said, pulling the backpack over his shoulder. He was two steps from the door, next to the Ganesh shrine, when the phone rang in the near empty lobby. Rang ominously. A female clerk answered.

"For you, Mr IBM," she called.

To his surprise it was Fernanda's voice on the line. "Oh

Randy, I'm so scared."

"Where are you? Don't worry, I have the money."

"I'm at the Delhi airport. What money? Oh Randy, they said he did it to himself. Mutilated himself! That these holy men hate their bodies. Hate their desires. But I don't think so, Randy. Win would never hurt himself like that. He was trying to help me. I think he was punished, Randy. By some awful force. For trying to help me!" Randy hears her sob. "It's this country, Randy. Dios mio! We need to leave this awful country!"

Randy did not understand a word of her babbling. He adjusted his backpack full of rupees. "So you are free? How did you get free?"

"Free from what, Randy? I'm just calling to let you know I arrive there in an hour. Can you meet me at the airport?"

"No!" Randy yelled. "No you mustn't come to Varanasi. You used to listen to me, used to do what I said. Please don't come to Varanasi. Book yourself into the hotel there in Delhi. The airport hotel. I will come for you. If not tonight, then tomorrow. Wait for me there!"

"But . . ."

"Don't question me! I'll explain it all later."

He hung up. My god, he thought, the fools haven't kidnapped my wife, they've kidnapped Julie!

41 Two Women Having A Chat

"Breathe deep," said Neelu, waving the pipe in front of her nose. "It's actually a good feeling, a kind of floating. You'll see."

Tied up as she was, in Neelu's apartment, Julie did as she was told. Still they continued to drug her, whenever she stirred. And with each breath of the thick smoke she felt her senses fading, her vision doubling and blurring. She could barely make out the card table and chairs that served as the dining area. She could just make out utensils hanging on the wall. What were they there for? Her mind spun. Getting no traction. Why was she being kept against her will?

Finally they helped her up, walked her out the door. Into a Varanasi she had not seen before, a place where the walls undulated and teethy sprites dashed before her, and the sun, when they came out of the shadows, the sun screamed at her to bow down.

She tried to speak but the words could not get past a thorny wall of vines growing in her brain. The thought came to her that she was dreaming, or that someone was dreaming her. I am electric, she said to herself, I am the sun. Bow down to me!

A bull stood on the sidewalk, stood blocking their way. Julie remembered him, reached to pet him, but she is pulled along, past the bull, guided down ghat steps to the river. Somehow she makes it down without falling head first. She smelled burned popcorn, as they sat her in a row boat next to the crematorium.

"Lean forward," a booming man's voice commanded. She leaned, and an elephant, yes, an elephant tied her waist to a large flat stone.

Neelu sat next to her, her arm around her, comforting her.

"You are so beautiful," Neelu told Julie, stroking her hair. "And you smell so nice. I wish I were as desirable as you."

Julie looked at Neelu, whose face was turning, before her eyes, into a dog's face. She tried to warn Neelu but no sound came.

"Don't worry," said Neelu. "Your husband is going to bring the money and we are all going to be rich. Mr Tishwali explained how the government deposit guarantee insurance will pay back all the money to the depositors. None of our customers will even know they were robbed. It will be as if there really were no robbery. While we split what was in the safe between ourselves."

The dog is barking at me, thought Julie. Trying to tell me something important. But I don't speak dog.

Neelu went on explaining how Mr Tishwali, sitting at the oars, was a great man, practically a god, to pull off such a grand illusion, but she might as well have been barking at the moon.

42 And He Did Nothing

Brahmin Brahma had let them slip past him. He'd sensed the time had come, and yet he did nothing. Only followed them to the top of the ghat, watched helplessly as the Frenchwoman, the fragile beauty, the one that shone with love, watched as she was tied to a deathstone. Watched as they rowed her out to the middle of the Ganges, where she would be fed to the turtles.

Had the time for him to act or not to act passed so quickly? Was he too late to help her? But if he did act, he would never reach Nirvana, Kali assured him of that.

He realized that this was the time of sacrifice, for great love, and turned his back on the scene. He went for a walk, to meditate on what to do next.

43 A Plan

Realizing it was Julie they had taken, and not Fernanda, Randy felt less guilty and a little more composed. He hoped that once he explained to Mr Tishwali that Julie was not his wife, they could reach a civil agreement on ending the whole charade. With the backpack full of rupees strapped on his back, he stopped at his hotel, on the way to the ghat, to figure out how to proceed without getting anyone killed.

What a thought – he, Randy – must come up with a plan that involved saving lives. His stomach knotted.

He was no bank robber. Neither was he some kind of hero. He was a programmer, for gosh sakes! The logic of 'If, Then, Else' was all he knew.

He opened the door to his room, slung off the heavy backpack onto the floor. He went in the bathroom, took a piss, and washed his face. The man in the mirror looked back without a hope. Randy returned to the bedroom, and as he did so he discovered a note on the floor.

Had they followed him? Slipped the note just now under the door?

But no, the note was not from the kidnappers, the note was from Julie. Her confession. He read it twice - how she had manipulated him, how she had played with his career, with his very life, by bringing him here to Varanasi. How she had hoped to have him all to herself, and so was crestfallen when she realized Fernanda had accompanied him. The note went on, explaining how Julie had tricked Fernanda into going alone to Rishikesh, so she could return to Varanasi and have Randy to herself. There was no mention in the note of her being kidnapped. He began to doubt that she had been.

He sat on the bed. Fought back a wave of nausea.

His chest hurt. A weight on his heart.

"What a fool I've been!"

He had dared to think that Julie's presence in India had been a gift from God. A gentle nudging. That she was the one. But no, nothing so magical. God had no hand in Julie's appearance. He should have known. This was all Julie's making. Julie's lie.

And this kidnap plot. This crazy bank robbing. Was there more to them? Were they only machinations of that bank manager and his partner? Or was Julie in on them too? Maybe they colluded to create this cruel joke? To ruin his career. His self respect. To make him lose Fernanda.

Fernanda, whose love flowed like the Ganges, encompassing him, carrying him away.

Julie, Julie whose love pounded him like heavy cold rain, forcing him to search for cover.

He felt his mind slipping. Going too far. Slow down. Slow down. Think logically. Logic is your core strength.

Don't start guessing. Confirm what was happening. What was truly being asked of him. What was real and what had he only imagined. He took off the bedspread, and dumped the money onto the bed, spilling half onto the floor. That was real, for sure. He took out the note Mr Tishwali gave him at the bank. That too was real and said exactly what he remembered.

He compared the handwriting in the ransom note to Julie's confession note. Even he could tell the difference in the writing style of the two notes. He could assume, then, that the notes were not written by the same person. His head hurt. He couldn't think this thing through. Was Julie behind the robbery as well? Had she brought him here to make love and then disgrace him by forcing him to rob his client's bank? Was this some cruel French revenge payback? To get back at him for breaking her heart in Paris? He tore up her note, and tossed aside the kidnap note.

I can play games too, he told himself. He filled the backpack with the bedspread, no rupees, and headed for Manikarnica Ghat to get to the bottom of this farce. To talk Mr Tishwali out of this horrible plan that could only ruin all their lives.

44 The Parley

Randy feels the heat from new bonfires, from new burning dead, covers his nose from the annoying smell as he reaches the partially submerged bottom step.

Asha is waiting for him in a small boat, with his severe look, in his holy golden robe. His face, his arms and his bare legs are freshly covered with ash and liquefied body fat from the burning dead. The stench coming off this man is more repulsive than the smell of the fires. No sign of Julie or Mr Tishwali.

"I need to know what's going on," Randy tells him.

"Get in," says Asha, brandishing a curved-blade gurkha knife. "We are headed there." He points with the knife towards the middle of the river.

Randy climbs aboard, spotting as he does the other boat. The boat with Mr Tishwali and Julie, and, is that Neelu?

For some reason seeing Neelu reassures him. He feels he has

come to know Neelu, working with her every day. Neelu wouldn't hurt a fly. Surely.

"So the plan was to have me rob the bank, take the blame, while you keep all the money?"

"Tishwali's plan, dear sir. I am just a pawn, same as you." Asha tries to smile, but on that narrow scarred face the affect is frightening. "Or perhaps you would call me a knight. An Aghori knight," says Asha, as he rows towards the other boat, the boat with Julie.

"What do you mean?" asks Randy, trying to connect with this kidnapper.

"Do you know what an Aghori is?" asks Asha.

"Not really," confesses Randy.

"An Aghori is a sadhu, an ascetic, who has reached a plateau of enlightenment. He has removed, through meditation and the breaking of taboos, the blinders men are born with, to see not only how things are but how they will become. For all is transient. Truth becomes lie, lie becomes truth, with the passing of time. The living all die, and the dead all come back to life. In time. This understanding gives us Aghoris power."

"The power to murder?" says Randy, deciding to take the offensive. "You killed that holy man who came to the bank and withdrew all that money, didn't you? I didn't imagine it. You burned him alive!"

Asha winces. "Oh so much you see and so little you understand. Yes I burned Sadhu Pratish, but only because he asked us to do so. To expunge his sin. He wanted to self-immolate, before he died a natural death, but he hadn't the courage. So my payment to him for going to the bank and pretending to be rich from his Ganesh Bank savings, my payment to him was to drug him and set him ablaze. To help him burn himself alive. To honor the Gods."

Randy feels sick. The boat rocks. The oars clunk and splash. They approach Mr Tishwali's anchored boat, the one with Julie and Neelu. "So you aren't a murderer? You won't hurt Julie?"

"Actually," says Asha, dropping the smile. "Our current plan might require one or more sacrifices. To bury the trail, so to speak, of your banditry. But these will be good deaths, if they must happen. You understand? Deaths that do honor to God Ganesh. For we shall build a huge new temple bank in his honor with the money you provide."

Randy's fists clinch. He thinks to jump the man, grab the knife next to him, but what would that get him? Julie at the bottom of the river, most likely. No he had to play along, watch for his chance.

Asha puts down the oars a minute. Holding the knife and a large chillum pipe in one hand, he lights the pipe with the other. He hands the warm pipe to Randy. "Please smoke this. It will make things easier."

Randy takes the pipe, but does not raise it to his lips.

"Please do as I say," says Asha. "We don't plan on killing you, if we don't have to. Just the opposite. Get you high, give you some of the money and let you go free. You might even make it back to the states. Wouldn't you like to go home with your wife?"

"Yes," says Randy. "More than anything in the world."

"Then smoke."

Randy takes a breath of the sweet bitter mix. He coughs.

"Again," says Asha, as he brings the boat alongside the other in the middle of the river, directly over the underwater cemetery of the innocents.

Randy looks at Julie, his poor lover, but she doesn't seem to recognize him. She's drugged. So she isn't in on this. Good. He notices too the rope around her waist, a rope that tied her to a large flat stone, a stone used to sink the dead. A deathstone.

"Hand me the backpack," says Mr Tishwali, eager to take a look, to crow victory. "Hand me the money." The fat man's eyes are glistening. He strokes his beard.

"What are you doing, Mr Tishwali?" Randy says. "Can't you see this is all a big mistake? You are holy men. Holy men don't do such things. And that woman, that woman you have there, all tied up, why, she isn't even my wife."

Mr Tishwali looks at Julie, frowns. "Are you saying you don't love this woman?"

Ah, there was the rub. Randy can't deny his feelings for Julie, even if such a denial would save her. For he did love Julie. He was in love with her. Despite everything. And his love for her meant the farce must go on.

He tosses the heavy pack into Mr Tishwali's boat, rocking both boats in the handoff.

Randy notices bubbles from the river, from below where the dead are being devoured, as Mr Tishwali unzips the backpack and pulls out the first of the bed cover. He gasps. Pulls and pulls and there is no end to it. Like a bad magic trick. There was no money in the pack, only the bed cover.

"Where is the money?!" he roars at Randy.

"No money?" asks Asha. He grabs the pipe from Randy who is pulling another long toke, giving himself over to the spirits.

Randy's head is clouded with smoke, like that first night at Mr Tishwali's house. At the party. From the smoke and too much confusing stimulus in a city as old as Death. These people had been his friends. How could they turn on him so? How could they be so heartless? He remembers his first night in bed with Julie – it had been a miracle to be with her again, to touch his skin to hers, to consummate what they had started years ago, even if it was a miracle of Julie's making.

He looks at her, all helpless in the other boat with Mr Tishwali and Neelu. Yes he is in love with her. And he is willing to die for her. He reaches a hand down to the surface, feels it move through his fingers, stealing away the remaining minutes of his life.

"I love this spot in the river," he says, rocking in rhythm with the gentle current. "Do you know what lies below us?"

"The dead," says Asha. "And you will join them if you do not tell us where you've hid the money."

"Turtles," says Randy. "Turtles all the way down." He laughs. Stands in the boat, spins around, almost goes over the side. Asha steadies him, forces him to sit back down. "You can't kill me," says Randy. "Not if you want to see the money. Millions of rupees. Millions!"

He turns to Julie. "Oh baby," he says. "Do you see the mess you've gotten us into?"

She recognizes him now. A tear appears and runs the smooth curve of her cheek.

"You shouldn't talk to your wife like that," says Neelu. "She's done no wrong."

"Oh if you only knew what she has done," says Randy. "And

she's not my wife! I told you. Never could be." He stopped himself. He'd gone too far. This was not the time or the place.

"All we want is the money," says Mr Tishwali. "And all the good it will bring."

"Free her then."

"First give us the money."

Randy fought the fog in his head. Yes. He must give them the money. They might let Julie go. They will kill him for sure but they might let Julie go.

"Julie won't be hurt?" he asks Neelu directly.

"I promise no harm will come to her," Neelu answers. "Your sacrifice will do much good, Randy. Think on that."

"My sacrifice, ha!" He tried to spit but the smoke had dried his mouth. "All right, then, take me ashore and I will bring the money."

Mr Tishwali nods to Asha, who pushes off, rowing Randy back to the ghat where three funeral pyres flare.

"Don't worry," Neelu says to Julie, in the gently rocking boat, as they wait for Randy's return with the cash. "I would die before I would let anything happen to one as beautiful as you. One who loves as truly as you."

45 Fernanda To The Rescue

At the Delhi airport, after hanging up the phone, Fernanda sits down on a plastic seat in the vast lobby, surrounded by a hundred other travelers, some sitting, some pulling luggage, herding kids, checking their tickets and the time, some grabbing a bite to eat. She thinks over all that Randy has said, and especially the way that he said it. He ignored her own horrifying story. Something is terribly wrong in Varanasi, she decides. Randy is in trouble. I can't stay here in Delhi. She takes out her ticket for Varanasi – checks the departure time. I must go there, she tells herself, I must go and help my husband.

So she takes the flight as planned, falling into a reverie as soon as they leave the ground. She daydreams about the day when Randy first came back into her life, eight years after she ran off with Chance and settled in the house next to the crystal mine in the Ouachita Mountains. He just called up one day, out of the blue, and invited himself to dinner.

They sat around the table, Chance, Fernanda and Randy.

"So how did you end up in Arkansas?" asked Randy.

"We needed a place to stay," said Chance. "I hoped my friend Noah could put us up. Which he did. You never met Noah?"

"No. I don't think so. Heard you talk about him. Where is he?"

"About a hundred miles west of here. In the Oklahoma State Penitentiary," said Chance. "In McAlester. Going on eight years. That's one reason we stayed, to help watch over things while he was away."

"And for the crystals," said Fernanda.

"That too," said Chance, giving Fernanda a sideways glance. He explained to Randy how Fernanda had realized Crystal Hill was ripe for mining. That she was the one responsible for them starting a crystal business. "She's a damn good wife," said Chance.

"I'm n . . ." Fernanda started to say but caught herself.

"So you're married?" Randy asked directly to Fernanda.

Not answering, she looked away.

"No, not married really," said Chance for her. "But we might as well be!" He got up to bring in dessert, fresh baked apple pie.

After lunch, Chance walked Randy up to the mine. Chance's

employee, an 18 year old kid, was inside the crater, near the flooded bottom, chipping out a foot wide plate sprouting elegant crystal points. Fernanda dashed out the back door and made her way barefoot through the tailings, over broken stone and thousands of crystal fragments, to the backside of the mine. She hid behind a quartz-veined boulder, within earshot of the two of them. Carefully, she peered around the edge with one eye.

"I didn't want to say anything," said Chance, "in front of the woman. But business isn't all that good right now."

"What's the matter?"

"Man, I don't know where to start. First off the Brazilians are flooding the market with product. Second, the hippie culture has mostly died in the states, except for Oregon and Washington State. I still get good orders from the northwest."

"What do hippies have to do with your business?"

"Oh, don't you know? Hippies believe crystals can heal you. But now all the hippies wear suits, drive Japanese cars, and see their parents' doctors. Over the years, they stopped believing and they stopped their buying."

"Hippies and Crystals," said Randy. "Cries and Whispers."

"What?"

"Nothin."

"And that rock store on the main road, we had to take out a mortgage to build it. A pretty penny to stock and then I have to pay someone to tend the place. And now, this past week, see all that water in the bottom of the pit?"

Randy looked again into the pit.

"Yes."

"We've reached the water line. We're a damn well, now, instead of a mine. It's a disaster."

"I see you have a tube going down, and a pump?"

"Yeah," said Chance. "We pump what we can, work a couple hours, then she fills back up."

"Why do you have to go so deep?"

"The deeper the vein, the bigger the crystals. Museums will pay top dollar for clusters of giant crystals. Sold one the other day for 60,000."

"Like the one I saw in Paris, I'll bet."

"What?"

"Yes. I saw one of your giant quartz pieces in Paris, in a rock shop at a flea market."

"Ah, I know who that would have been. I even remember the cluster. Had one fat scepter crystal, looked kinda like a ..."

"Yes that's the one," said Randy and they both laughed.

Suddenly Chance turned to Randy, grabbed him by the shoulders and blurted, "Man, I never wanted to leave you on that road. I never wanted to leave you."

Fernanda strained to see the expression on Randy's face. She could practically feel the emotion building up inside of him. She wanted to leave her hiding place, run to him, tell him how sorry she was, but she could not.

"That's ok," Randy said, passing his hand over his face. "Things have worked out. I'm better for it actually."

"She told me to leave you, Randy. Freddy told me, *Vamanos!*"

Randy pulled back. Fernanda read anger in the way he moved. "Chance, I understand. I do. I don't want to hear any more on the subject."

He turned and headed back down to the house alone. Settled himself in a rocker on the porch, rocking slowly, hand to his chin.

A hummingbird zoomed under the porch, drank from a feeder hanging down low. A second hummingbird appeared. Randy watched the two of them zip one way and the next, forwards and backwards, as the sky turned a rusty yellow. Wisps of dirty clouds crossed the horizon, catching the sun, glowing pink.

"Why are you here?" She asked the back of his head through

the screen door. "After so many years, why now? Why?"

Randy did not turn around. But he did stop rocking. He must be thinking, is she alone? Is Chance in earshot? Fernanda felt a strange wetness under her feet. She stepped aside – saw the bloody prints she'd left.

"I came to see you," he said, with a wave of his hand. Still he did not turn to face her. How much time did they have left, to speak like this, alone? "I was in this store in Paris and suddenly I remembered you kissing me, how good that felt you kissing me, and I decided I needed to see you again." He told her this as a little boy would confess his secret crush.

"You should go," she told him.

He stood up. He would not face her.

"I brought you a present from Paris," he said with a breaking voice. He walked down the porch steps. "I left it on the chair."

He climbed into his Honda. Sat there for a long moment. Fernanda came out on the porch, wanting to catch him. Wanting to tell him that she was sorry, that she had made the mistake of her life that night she chose Chance over him. Randy glanced towards her, from the driver's seat. She saw, felt, the expression in his crestfallen face. The engine came on with a roar, the car's tires spun. "*Vamanos!*" she thought she heard him yell as his car swerved and disappeared down the grooved road between the oak trees, racing away from her, leaving her bleeding on the front porch to Chance.

She had braced herself on the porch rail, bleeding on the inside as well, sure she would never see Randy again. But then not 2 months later Chance got Crystal pregnant. Noah's no good daughter. Randy heard about the affair, and came running to console Fernanda. He helped her through that difficult time, and finally, irrevocably, she fell for him head over heels. He needed her now, in Varanasi, she was sure of it. She would come and stand by his side.

The plane lands. Fernanda grabs one of the death-defying taxis at the Varanasi airport, puts up with the nerve-wracking, honk-filled ride into town, and enters the hotel.

She walks the wooden stairs, makes her way down the crooked hallway, opens the door to their room, and exclaims, "*Ay Chihuahua!*" The bed is piled three feet high with thousands of bills. Notes of 100, 500 and 1000 rupees. She walks over and touches the money. Drops her bag. Closes the door quickly - before someone else sees. What is going on here! *Que pasa!* She looks about the room for some clue, some explanation. Finally she finds the kidnap note next to the bed, picks it up and reads it aloud.

"We have your spouse. Withdraw all the money and bring it to us in the backpack provided to Manikarnica Ghat. Or something terrible might happen."

Dios mio. They've kidnapped Randy!

She looks for the backpack mentioned in the note, but finds none. So instead she empties her travel bag and stuffs it with money. She stuffs a pillowcase and her purse with rupees as well, as much as she can carry. She hides the rest in the closet. She leaves the room with the cash, locks the door, turns the knob to make sure it is locked securely, then jogs down the hall, outside the hotel, down the river steps, directly for the cremation ghat.

"I hope I am not too late!"

46 A Desparate Plan

Meanwhile, after persuading Asha to wait for him below, Randy has run up the ghat steps not fifty yards from where Fernanda is heading down. He reaches the hotel, his heart pounding. Will they kill me, he wonders. Even if I give them the cash?

He takes the hotel stairs two at a time, runs the leaning hallway, unlocks the door to his room, and stops short.

How is this possible?

The money is gone! Every last bill!

I've been robbed!

What, what am I to do? How can I save Julie now?

Think Randy think! You with your logical brain, compute the answer to this problem. And quickly now, quickly, they will not wait long!

He envisions the spot where they have Julie, in the river, above the underwater cemetery. He knows the place well. He could dive from shore, swim under them, surprise them and free Julie somehow.

Yes. He could attempt that, with scuba gear. What choice did he have, now that the money was gone?

He burst back out the door and raced himself down the ghat steps to where Raj kept the air tanks and scuba gear, all the while staying low and steering clear of Asha still waiting, shoreside, in the rowboat, for his return.

47 The Time Has Come

Earlier that afternoon, when Brahmin Brahma noticed a drugged Julie being guided down the ghat steps to the boat, when he saw her struggle as they tied her to a deathstone, he realized the time had come for him not to act, if he hoped to reach Nirvana.

Too though he realized that this was the time of sacrifice, for great love. He knew why he had been asked not to interfere. The Gods would have their way. And that made him angry. So be it.

48 A Good Sacrifice

Fernanda tires, halfway down the steps, carrying all the money. She walks the rest of the way, reaches the ghat of the burning dead just as the sun begins to set. She calls out, "I am here! I have the money! Don't kill my Randy!"

She turns in every direction, hollering, showing a handful of money. Pilgrims start to crowd her.

Asha stands in the boat. Who is this woman? Did Mr Randy send her in his stead? He climbs from the boat, strides up and grabs her by the arm.

"Shut up!" he tells her. "Where is Mr Randy?"

"That's what I want to know," she tells this strange thin holy man covered in ash and smelling like the dead.

"Who are you?" He demands of her.

"I am Randy's wife," she tells him.

The look on his face. As if he were about to cry.

"But, we kidnapped you," says Asha.

"You never kidnapped me," says Fernanda.

"The other you. His wife."

"There is no other me. There is only me," says Fernanda. "*Yo soy la unica.*"

"But I saw with my own eyes, the love they had for each other. I saw them kiss!"

Fernanda notices a boat some ways off, a man in a white suit, with two women. One of the women looks familiar. Slumped against a special back support, is that Julie? A picture begins to form.

"Are you saying you kidnapped Randy's old friend?" she asks the man, "because you thought she was me?"

"I'm not sure what to think anymore," says Asha. "Maybe she is you. And you are pretending to be her? All I know is that you, whoever you are, need to come with me. Along with all this money."

He starts to drag her and the money towards his boat.

From atop the ghat temple, Lord Hanuman with his pet goat and Kali with her dead cat watch the show. Are any of us who we think we are? Lord Hanuman asks his goat. I am, says the goat.

Just then, from a small gap at the top of the ghat, Brahmin Brahma, the enlightened bull, comes hustling down towards Fernanda, followed by a herd of black water buffalo. The scene, as Fernanda and Asha look up, is impressive. Overwhelming. A stampede heading right towards them.

No! cries Kali from the temple top. I told him No No NO! Lord Hanuman, the monkey God, the incarnation of Shiva, laughs quietly.

49 Breaking Taboo

The buffalo rush down the steps, separating a frightened Asha and Fernanda, knocking Asha into the river and Fernanda on her back on the steps. A pillowcase full of money floats off. Asha struggles after it, between the buffalo, on tiptoe, he cannot swim. He manages to grab the pillowcase full of thousand rupee bills, and turns towards shore, to the safety of the steps, when something clamps onto his bare leg and holds him fast. He cries out.

"Let go!"

The thing will not let go. He reaches down, underwater, his hand discovers a hard and heavy shell, the shell of some creature. A god? The creature moved then, pulling away from shore, pulling hard, forcing Asha into deeper water, forcing his head into the water, an inch at a time. No this can't be happening, he tells himself. He struggles against the creature, breaks surface for a moment.

"Oh God! Help me!"

Pulled under again, by what must be a demon, Asha's mouth and nose just below the surface, his eyes just above. He spots Fernanda on the steps, pleads for her to help, but his words are swallowed by the river. His lungs demand air but he can only gulp water. He lets go the pillowcase full of money, of all things material. His eyes go sad, nostalgic, taking in as they do, one last time, his beloved Manikarnica Ghat, with its temples and its smoldering dead.

On the river's edge, Fernanda, who cannot swim, yells at the bystanders to save Asha. But the locals know better. Aghori sadhus like Asha, who prove their holiness by sinning, are not to be trusted. Not even when they claim they are drowning.

The pillowcase full of money, on the other hand, draws much sympathy, and is quickly rescued. Fernanda argues that she is the rightful owner, and eventually, with the intervention of various holy men, the pillowcase full of money is returned to her.

50 Falling For You

Without his wetsuit, swimming deep so as not to be spotted, Randy felt bitterly cold. He tried to create as few bubbles as possible as he came up along their anchor line, his body shivering. The air tank he'd taken wasn't full, but should last long enough for him and Julie to make shore unseen.

The trick was freeing her. If he came up alongside, they would be on him long before he could cut the cord around her.

The anchor line jerked. No! They were weighing anchor, about to leave. This couldn't be! With the current and Tishwali rowing, he wouldn't be able to keep up.

Why were they leaving? Had they given up on him bringing the money already?

He let out the pressured air in his lungs and swam fast as he could for the boat some twenty feet above him. He broke surface like a shark, shooting up, and as he did so he grabbed hold of the stone Julie was tied to.

The stone toppled over the edge of the boat, falling into the water with Randy, pulling Julie along with it, and Neelu, who at the last second grabbed onto Julie's blouse. They made a huge splash and plummeted together to the bottom far below.

Randy kept his hold on the rock that held Julie, and struggled to pressurize his ears which were screaming with the air being squeezed out of his sinuses.

51 All Alone

The splash from their fall soaked the back of Mr Tishwali's white suit. He turned around, dropped the anchor line, started to jump in himself, to save Neelu, but too late. They were already gone to the depths of the river. The deathstone assured their end. The water calmed and the boat stilled. A minute later it was as if they had never been in the boat. As if they had never even been alive.

"Neelu . . ."

His head spun. He fell back on his seat in the boat. He felt sick, but he would not give in to the feeling. "I will prevail," he told himself. "Ganesh will see me through this."

Mr Tishwali wiped his eyes and turned to see what was going on at the ghat. He watched as the water buffalo came out of the river, one by one, and headed back up the wide steps, to go graze the piles of trash in the city streets. He saw no sign of Asha. Only that woman, collecting her scattered belongings. Who was that woman; why had Asha struggled with her? Why had she been of interest to Asha?

Where was dear Asha? And where was Mr Randy with the money? None of this made any sense!

52 The Sacrifice

Neelu held tight to Julie and closed her eyes, as they plummeted through layers of colder and colder water. A tiny scream began in her ears, like a tea kettle going off in a distant room, only with the sound came pain. A demoness shreaking in her ears! Louder and louder the deeper they sank. Trying to get out! Oh what pain in her ears! Still she would not let go of Julie. She had promised she would protect her with her life, and so she hung on as they fell through the depths.

They hit bottom. The screaming resided. Her world grew quiet. Quieter than she'd ever known. Neelu opened her eyes. Through the murky water, with the last of the sun, she could just make out a skeleton hand, a molting arm, a field of bones. They had reached the world of the dead.

Bubbles. She looked down. Randy? He was pushing a tube into Julie's mouth. More bubbles. With his free hand he sawed with a small knife at Julie's bonds. In a second she was free of the rope.

Randy reached up with the air tube and pushed it into Neelu's mouth.

Air! Wonderful air. She took two deep breaths, smiled at Randy and Julie, then let the tube go, pushing off towards the surface some 60 feet above them. Julie would be alright with Randy. She had kept her promise and made her safe. Now she could return to her life on the surface with Mr Tishwali.

Randy opened his mouth wide, as if he were trying to yell, but all she noticed was a mouthful of bubbles as she kicked towards the surface, holding the compressed air in her lungs with all her strength.

Strange, how she felt, as she approached the surface, traveling so fast, she was practically flying.

Three feet from the surface her lungs, full of compressed air, exploded in her chest, bursting like overfilled balloons.

She reached the surface, reached all that wonderful air in the world of the living, but it did her no good, for she was already of the dead.

From the bottom Randy watched as Neelu's body, high above, began to spasm. The body went limp then and hung, just below the surface, as if on an invisible line. Holding Julie tightly, so she wouldn't make the same deadly mistake of rushing to the surface, he guided her slowly up and towards shore, sharing the last of the air with her.

53 Nirvana

Night has fallen in Varanasi. In old town a girl stands in the middle of the street in front of a black and white bull with a sloping hump on his back. The girl is Kali, Goddess of black fire, the bull is Brahmin Brahma.

"You had to interfere!?" the girl yells at the bull, standing in his usual place in a street where everyone knows and admires him, a street where he stands every day oblivious to the honking and near misses of the passing cars and tuktuks and motorbikes. She places a red dot of her blood on his forehead.

"I had to take a bath, that's all," says Brahmin Brahma, speaking through the magic of that dot.

"With a herd of buffalo?"

"A chance meeting of old friends."

"If I have my say, you will live again," threatens Kali, full of spite. "I think next time you will be reborn as a turtle, feeding at the bottom of the Ganges on rotting flesh. On the flesh of that girl Neelu."

"Then so be it," said Brahmin Brahma. He turned his head from her, into oncoming headlights, where the grill of a speeding truck struck a death blow on the red dot between his eyes, cracking his skull, releasing his soul.

But he did not come back as a turtle. No, Brahmin Brahma did not come back at all.

He went free.

54 That Ends Well

Julie flew back alone to France, for the operation on her shredded eardrums. They gave her a 50-50 chance of hearing once again.

Randy felt terrible. Maybe he shouldn't have tried to save Julie by pulling her in like that, the quick descent destroying her ears. His own ears were hurt, though he had mitigated the damage by swallowing and wiggling his jaw all the way down. Time should heal his wounds.

At least he'd been careful bringing her to the surface, giving their bodies enough time to adjust to the change in pressure, making sure she exhaled the compressed air from his tank. At least he hadn't destroyed her lungs as well.

Her heart? He wasn't so sure he'd been careful enough with her heart.

Fernanda sleeps on the flight, her head on Randy's shoulder. Randy likes her there, next to him, and only occasionally, on the flight, and later settled back into his life at home in Arkansas, does he remember the hunger in Julie's kisses, in Varanasi and Khajuraho, and sigh.

Postword

Most of the money Fernanda took to the river was recovered and returned to the bank. What little loss that occurred was covered by the government insurance, as Mr Tishwali had envisioned. The body of Mr Tishwali's partner, Asha, was never found. Neelu's body was recovered and she was given the proper ceremonial burning for someone of her caste.

Mr Tishwali himself, after a minor breakdown, pleaded at his civil trial that it was all a grand misunderstanding; that the whole act had been a fake robbery to test the new banking system he'd purchased from IBM.

"This is all an illusion," he pleaded on the stand. "Nothing is real." Real or not, he was forced to sell his ownership in the bank, and held civilly liable for the accidental death of Neelu. He had to forfeit the proceeds of the sale of his First National Bank of Ganesh to Neelu's grieving parents and a few elders in the order of the Aghori sadhus that had helped him acquire the temple in the first place.

After the trial, Mr Tishwali and his wife moved to Mumbai where his wife opened a small store that sold fine silk saris and colored scarves. Mr Tishwali stopped wearing his famous white suit, he preferred a dark suit now. He spent most of his time walking the streets, thinking about what could have been if only the Gods had been on his side. His wife asked if she could put a shrine to Ganesh in front of the store, but Mr Tishwali forbade her.

The only criminal investigation tied, if indirectly, to these events, involved the recent serial castrations and murders that occurred in Varanasi and Rishikesh. The Indian police, after questioning the yoga teacher who was viciously attacked at Harmony House, filed a petition with the FBI requesting an international person of interest warrant for one Mexican-American named Fernanda, maiden name Guadalupe de Cortez.

On his return home, Randy took time off from work and kept busy helping his best friend Chance pry crystal clusters from their quartz mine in Arkansas. Numerous requests flooded in for his services at IBM, once word got out that he had thwarted not only a devious kidnapping but a sophisticated embezzlement scheme during his last project in India. A colleague emailed that Randy was now considered to be IBM's 007. He could name his project anywhere in the world.

Randy didn't give a damn. He worried over Julie. Was her operation a success? She didn't answer his emails. Wouldn't pick up his calls (could she not hear the ring?). Finally he contacted her manager, who told Randy that Julie had recovered most of her hearing, but had taken a 3 month leave with no means to contact.

Fernanda made a new friend the other day at the riding club. Kalene is her name. Twenty-something, dressed in a yesteryear style, she surprised Fernanda with the confession that, although she had seduced many men, she had never been in love. "What's it like to fall in love?" she asked Fernanda, looking at her with her exotic yet strangely familiar eyes. "You know, don't you? Could you teach me how?"

Meanwhile, back in Varanasi, Lord Hanuman and his all devouring goat continue their vigil. They spend their days philosophizing about life and pondering Kali's mysterious disappearance, while God, the Beginning and the End, continues expanding in all directions, looking for love, imagining what it must be like, living out the possibilities through us his children.

Bathing with the Dead

About The Author

Software developer and dreamer of stories. Like most fiction writers Else's interest in writing began when he discovered books that talked to him, between the lines, books whose authors (spirits, invisible) sparked a conversation that the spirit in him could only respond to by writing stories himself. For other spirits. A daisy chain conversation.

Married, with 4 grown kids and 11 grandkids. Enjoys traveling the world to visit friends and find new stories, occasionally rock-hounds – as shared on his website, rayelse.com.

You may contact Else at rayelsemail@gmail.com.

ELSE

By Else

The First Kiss Series

Bathing with the Dead

Her Heart in Ruins (available Dec 2015)

All that we touch (available June 2016)

More to come . . .

Also in the works

My Father's Lies

ELSE

Made in the USA
Charleston, SC
13 July 2015